MEGIS

MEGIS

Michael Genrich

iUniverse, Inc.
New York Lincoln Shanghai

MEGIS

iUniverse books may be ordered through booksellers or by contacting:

iUniverse
2021 Pine Lake Road, Suite 100
Lincoln, NE 68512
www.iuniverse.com
1-800-Authors (1-800-288-4677)

The locations described herein exist today as depicted, and all are readily accessible to any casual visitor to Michigan's Upper Peninsula. All characters, however, are completely fictional. Any resemblance to any person, living or dead, is purely coincidental.

ISBN-13: 978-0-595-38542-3 (pbk)
ISBN-13: 978-0-595-82922-4 (ebk)
ISBN-10: 0-595-38542-7 (pbk)
ISBN-10: 0-595-82922-8 (ebk)

Printed in the United States of America

For Victoria, my partner in life, without whose support this book could not have been written.

PROLOGUE

▼

It would be another hot day, the man at the wheel in the pilothouse amidships of the fish tug thought, on that late June day in 1953; the third in a row of bright, brassy, one hundred degree days, days that baked his fisherman's pale skin to a rosy red as it reflected off the calm surface of the big lake. It was unseasonably warm for so early in the summer, he reflected ruefully, at least for Ontonagon, hard against the south shore of Lake Superior in Michigan's western Upper Peninsula. The wind was out of the south, as it had been for the previous several days, and the flies would be bad again, he knew; stable flies blown out of Wisconsin by the stiff south breeze, as all the local folk assumed, vicious, persistent pests that savaged every exposed knuckle, knee and ankle, where a man's skin was stretched tightly across the bone. The woods were already tinder dry, and a forest fire like the many previous ones that had shaped so much of Ontonagon's past and topography was a very real possibility.

The fish tug *Anna M.* was running straight out from the Ontonagon harbor that lay astern of the fifty-foot long steel-hulled boat, and the lighthouse on the south shore of the river mouth was still in view. The muddy tongue of the river, always the color of milk-and-coffee regardless of the season, lapped at the flanks of the big tug, with its ponderous current being blown unusually straight out into the big lake by the southerly breezes of the past several days and with its waters a murky stain upon the surrounding azure surface of Lake Superior. The dull plume of the tired, silt-laden river would travel for miles, as it always did, while all the time pouring its turgid contents into the icy, crystalline waters, before it finally succumbed to dilution by the largest freshwater lake in the world.

And, as he often did on the way to the fishing grounds, in the wasted time necessary to reach his nets at the tug's top speed of ten knots, the tired, middle-aged man at the wheel of the tug speculated idly on what had ever possessed his parents to immigrate to these fly-blown shores from the ancestral island of their fishermen family in the Bay of Bothnia on the Baltic Sea, a bay tucked tightly between Sweden and Finland on the fringe of the Arctic Circle some twenty degrees further north in latitude than even this northerly place in Michigan's Upper Peninsula. How difficult could it have been for his ancestors, he wondered, to fish as long as one wanted into the long daylight night of midsummer, knowing that rest would come during the long winter hours when the sun was extinguished, and when travel to the mainland could only be accomplished by sled drawn by reindeer over the sea ice? Sitting by the fire surrounded by family, and telling stories about the summer's fishing and the old days, and eating warm meals, and repairing nets and gear for the next season? Sleeping in a warm bed with his wife, and playing with his children, and making more children as often as possible? But whenever he had spoken of this in this way to his father, Johannes Bergstrom, the old man would just cluck his tongue, and smile slightly, and shake his head, and say nothing.

No rest for him, Marcus Bergstrom, would come next winter, he reflected; no, for him, life was one long day after another long day, every day, all year long, and once the fishing gear was repaired and put away for the winter and the *Anna M.* laid up, it would be time to make ice.

The Bergstroms, the father and sons, made ice with a big circular saw, a saw with an air-cooled engine that was mounted on a sled. They made a thousand twenty by twenty-inch blocks of sixteen to thirty-inch thick river ice each day, all winter long, to supply their own and the other Ontonagon fishermen's icehouses. In the icehouses, the ice would be stacked and packed in sawdust from a sawmill some distance from town, insulating the icy mass for the upcoming season.

In addition to preserving their own fish, the Bergstrom icehouse supplied two tons of ice each day all summer long for the *Chippewa*, the Chicago, Milwaukee and St. Paul passenger train that took the fishermen's catch from the Ontonagon depot to the market in Chicago; and four to five tons of ice per week to the Northern Lumber Company for their refrigerator cars taking meat and other perishables to their logging camps; and to stores and saloons throughout Ontonagon County. But that was months away, Marcus knew, and now it was time to fish.

Marcus Bergstrom briefly allowed himself a moment of self-pity as the *Anna M.* plowed through the quiet waters, its surface only slightly rippled by the early morning southerly breeze. But time was precious, and he had little of it for introspection, save for these morning runs to his nets.

His father, Johannes, had died the previous summer at age seventy-seven. The leathery fisherman had put in the same long days as his sons, every day, until the very week before his death. It had been, Marcus reflected, as if the old man had finally worn out, like one of the old cotton nets they had used before the advent of modern nylon. For his part, at age forty-four, Marcus already felt like an old man.

Marcus' two older brothers were more and more preoccupied with the other aspects of the family business and ever less able to help him with the fishing. He had no sons of his own, and he was ever more reliant on shore hands and transient help to assist him each day on the lake. He loved his wife and three daughters, Marcus reflected morosely as he gazed ahead at the vast freshwater sea before him, but it would surely be a help to have someone to count on out here. Superior looked like a millpond this morning to his practiced eye, but he knew that it could become a raging monster before the safety of the river could be achieved; and the river was the only safe harbor for many miles in either direction. At least, he could use someone more reliable than this drunken red *Indiansk*, he thought darkly, as he stared briefly from behind at the broad back of the large dark man who squatted at the bow of the *Anna M.* like a silent stone figurehead in his ragged, scavenged clothes.

The Indian was monitoring their progress with his gaze fixed on the western horizon as if searching for something; his long, matted black hair stirred only slightly in the morning breeze. No one knew who the Indian was, or what his name was, or where he came from, or where he went in the wintertime.

Those in the village who thought of the man at all supposed that he was a last relic, a holdout, of an Ojibwa band that had had a permanent summer settlement on the south side of the Ontonagon River mouth from before the white man arrived in the area in the mid-1840's. The rest of the band had all either fled to relatively more favorable areas such as Baraga to the east and Odanah to the west or had intermarried with the local white settlers, to become the homogenized 'Finndians' who now populated a great deal of Ontonagon County.

All anyone knew of the Indian for certain was that he slept in the alleys and the doorways of the village during the warm months and that he stayed as drunk as possible at all times. He would occasionally rouse himself long enough to do yard work, such as raking or splitting wood for the local homeowners, for either food or spare change; or he would wander down to the fish houses on the east bank of the river, where the slough dumped into the main branch, in the early morning to see if anyone needed a deck hand that day. He would make just enough money to purchase a bottle or two from one of the local saloons, establishments that were never particular about who they sold to as long it was at the back door that abutted the alley.

But mostly, the Indian was harmless and unobtrusive, the local citizenry thought, just another anonymous casualty like the other men that this Ontonagon country had chewed up and spit out. Legions of them who had cut the trees and mined the ground had a story to tell that no one particularly wanted to hear; innocuous additions to a tired, worn-down village that had witnessed far more tragedies than most Upper Michigan towns of similar age.

And so the Indian had come to be on the *Anna M.* this morning. Marcus Bergstrom had already resigned himself that he would be going out alone this day, for his brothers were delivering ice. All of the usual shore hands were still drinking and debauching away their big paychecks from the Jewish holidays of earlier in the month.

Jewish customers in Chicago and New York paid the highest prices for Lake Superior fish, which were considered to be the finest in the world, and they often paid double the going market rate on the major Jewish holidays. Moreover, the fishermen's workload was lightened considerably since the fish had to be shipped to the Jewish market 'in the round', or whole, as they had to be blessed by a rabbi before cleaning and dressing. These holidays were a godsend to the Ontonagon fishermen, and each fish house on the river displayed a current Jewish calendar in a prominent location to remind them of these banner paydays.

The immediate prospect of a day alone on the big lake was not particularly alarming to Bergstrom; he often went out by himself, although his workload was then dramatically increased with no one to help. Also, the shift to the hot weather fishery was underway, due to the early summer, and the Ontonagon fishermen were enjoying a momentary lull in the frenetic pace of the brief fishing season.

The catch from the near-shore four and a half-inch gillnets in Union Bay and west of Green that had yielded a spring bounty of whitefish and lake trout, the trout running two to one over the whitefish, had slowed to a trickle. These nets had already been pulled and would be repaired for the summer deep-water sets and fall fishing.

On this day, Bergstrom had only to pull a single gang of one and a quarter-inch linen gillnets that was set in two hundred fifty feet of water for bloater chubs towards Gull Point. The 'bloats', the tiniest members of the whitefish genus at eight to nine inches long, would be cut in half diagonally and used as bait for deepwater hook line fishing for lake trout, in water as deep as seven hundred feet, all summer and fall.

In November, the 'herring', another somewhat larger member of the whitefish clan, at twelve to fifteen inches, that is sometimes known as 'Menominee' in other parts of Michigan, would return to the shallow near-shore waters between the Ontonagon pier and the Big Cranberry River to spawn. Then the gillnetting would begin again until the river became icebound and impassable. The Bergstroms then became what were whimsically known locally as 'herring chokers', a term that accurately describes the method of squeezing a herring through the mesh opening of a gill net, until fishing was no longer possible due to the winter.

Marcus saw the Indian approach long before he reached the Bergstrom dock, since except for him the riverfront was deserted this morning. Poor bastard must be broke again, Marcus thought judgmentally. A simple "Hey, you!" and a beckoning wave of the arm from Bergstrom was enough of a contract to engage the man for the day.

Bergstrom had hired the Indian occasionally, during the dark man's rare sober moments, for he was as strong as an ox and the best knife man that the son of the Swedish immigrants had ever seen. Marcus Bergstrom, of 'Bergstrom and Sons Fish Company, Ontonagon, Michigan', was always short-handed. With the Indian on board, one almost didn't need the mechanical lifter to raise the nets or winch in the hook lines.

The average daily lift of five hundred to six hundred pounds of trout and whitefish was almost always gutted and cleaned under the Indian's flying knife by the time that the fish tug had pulled into the river channel on the way back to the Bergstrom dock. A million gulls would be diving and squabbling in their wake over the offal that the man who cleaned the fish pitched through the side door back by the stern. Too bad, Marcus had always thought with some regret, one never knew when, or even if, the Indian would show up in the morning.

But for all of his introspection as the *Anna M.* plowed through the easy morning waves of Lake Superior, Marcus Bergstrom was not particularly unhappy with his lot in life this late June day in 1953. He had a fine, attractive, and strong wife who was a good cook. His three daughters doted on him, and they all had a warm, well-built two-story house in a pleasant lakeshore village

The village had literally resurrected itself from the ground up after a devastating fire that had completely destroyed it almost sixty years earlier. It had an efficient infrastructure, a small but functional hospital, and a good school system, all of which were important things to immigrant families.

Marcus Bergstrom had been exempt from the draft during World War II, even though he had been of draft age and in top physical condition, since he was part of the small male population left in the country whose job it was to feed the rest of the United States. He had been able to raise his family in relative peace and security and tend to the family business, with only occasional guilt pangs about the childhood friends who had come back to Ontonagon County maimed from the conflicts in Europe and the Pacific, or who hadn't come back at all.

As the *Anna M.* plowed along to the two hundred fifty-foot depth contour, where Bergstrom would alter course to the southwest for the ten-mile run to where his nets were set off Gull Point, the southerly breeze freshened as the sun came up behind them, and the blue haze of the exhaust from the big one hundred horsepower Kahlenberg oil engine propelling the fish tug that had enveloped them since leaving the river finally dissipated. Bergstrom did not notice the change in the air. It was as if the smell of diesel oil was trapped in the very steel hull of the ship, and in all his clothes and gear, and in the innermost fiber of his being.

The odor was as much a part of Bergstrom as the skin of his body, and it had been ever since the fish tug had been built specifically for the Bergstroms several years previously in Manitowoc, Wisconsin to replace their older and smaller gasoline-powered boat. The *Anna M.* was state-of-the-art for a Great Lakes fishing vessel; but in the stores, the public buildings, and on the street, everyone knew that a diesel fishing boat sailor was in the vicinity by his distinctive aroma, even if he was freshly bathed.

As Bergstrom now altered the tug's course to the southwest, the only reaction of the Indian in the bow was to slightly shift his gaze, as if keeping some distant vision seen only by him in view. Bergstrom knew from experience that the large dark man would remain like this, inert and silent, until the nets were reached. When action on his part was required, the Indian would only speak in monosyllables, and he would move through his tasks with an economy of motion. It was part and parcel of the man and completely unnoticeable to Bergstrom, for it was as much a characteristic of the Indian as the fisherman's peculiar diesel odor was to himself.

Even as he altered course, Bergstrom could see the black veil of clouds forming on the western horizon, and in short order he could hear the faint rumble of thunder, far away. The sky was quickly darkening. The wind switched suddenly to the northwest, chilling his bare flesh that, conditioned by the warm weather, was now unaccustomed to the abruptly cold breeze.

This was going to be a close thing, Bergstrom thought, grimly. They might just have enough time to get the nets aboard without picking out the bloats and make it back to the river before the storm was upon them. Bergstrom pushed the engine throttle forward as far as possible and strained his eyes, searching through the quickening froth for the black and white double-flagged buoy at the shoreward end of his nets.

By the time they had arrived at the fishing area off Gull Point, the *Anna M.* was rolling heavily in the high seas that now cut across her bow. The sky was as black as night. Bergstrom momentarily considered giving the day up as a very bad idea when, suddenly, his shoreward buoy came into view, close aboard.

The *Anna M.* was a very seaworthy boat, Bergstrom knew from long experience, and virtually unsinkable when lightly loaded. So, against his better judgment and to save another trip, he pulled abreast of the buoy, upwind where they would be able to hook the lead line and pull in the net before the wind blew them off the spot.

Lightning was now tearing jagged streaks in the dark velvet horizon. The thunderclaps were coming quickly, with no discernable pause between the strike and the reverberation. Even the Indian in the bow finally stirred himself, knowing that quick action would be required on his part.

As Bergstrom backed the tug down to slow its forward progress abreast of the buoy, a particularly spectacular lightning bolt split the black sky to the southwest over Gull point. A bright flare seared the horizon as the bolt struck an enormous white pine on the shore. The big old pine, being tinder-dry and full of pitch, exploded in a towering pillar of flame, a beacon against the sky that was visible for miles around.

At the strike, the Indian in the bow jerked towards the flaming torch on the horizon as if struck with an electric prod. He stood transfixed, staring at the scene.

"*Megis!*" the dark man shouted loudly into the howling wind, as the tug came to a brief stop, rolling wildly in the waves, with its engine in neutral. The word was understood only by him and was heard by no one save him.

"*MEGIS!*" the Indian screamed into the tumult, bracing himself against the gunwales in the bow, as Bergstrom swung wildly for the net lead with a boathook. The fisherman missed badly, and then he plunged awkwardly head first into the icy waters, propelled by a particularly violent wave.

"*MEE-GISS!*" the Indian implored his *Anishinabe* spirit ancestors in despair as he beheld the distant flaming visage. He desperately clung to the bow light staff as the tug was blown quickly downwind, like a leaf skittering across the wave tops.

Bergstrom floundered in the water next to his net buoy and waved his arms desperately before submerging beneath the towering waves, never to reappear. For, like many other Ontonagon fishermen, Marcus Bergstrom had never learned how to swim.

The *Anna M.* was found washed up on the beach some two miles west of the Ontonagon pier head the next morning, abandoned but completely intact. No trace of Marcus Bergstrom was ever found. The Indian was never seen again in the village of Ontonagon, and no one particularly noticed his absence.

CHAPTER 1

▼

"*Blin*, it's cold!" muttered *Ryadovoi* Fyodor Bogdanskii to himself, for-lornly, as the eighteen-year-old Russian Army private absent-mindedly contemplated yet another trek on foot around the compound. It was 0300 on January 8, 1998, a date and time that the young man had just noted laboriously in pencil in stilted, unpracticed Cyrillic text on the tattered round sheet. The mimeographed sheet, in front of a hundred other tat-tered sheets, all barely constrained on the fifty-year-old clipboard by the weak spring clip, was barely legible.

It had been only six months since Bogdanskii's conscription into the Red Army. But already, he knew instinctively without calculation, he had made this same circuit several hundred times.

The young soldier readjusted the weight of the heavy Mosin-Nagent bolt-action rifle slung across his shoulder with a shrug. The practiced move was unconscious, to better carry the weapon with which he guarded the gray concrete compound against an unknown outside threat that even he knew would probably never come, even in his simple-minded view of the world. The shrug was similar to that mannerism which indelibly iden-tified Bogdanskii as being Russian without his ever realizing it: the eternal subjection of mere flesh to fate, as much of a national characteristic in his vast country as the upraised middle finger of more passionate regions.

It can be no more than zero degrees centigrade, Bogdanskii thought to himself. Worse, it had snowed at least twenty centimeters several hours previously, in this area unaccustomed to snow: the gently rolling plain of West European Russia, only several kilometers from the border with the Ukraine.

The thin young soldier hiked up the throat of his overly large greatcoat around his sallow neck, where the whiskers poked up here and there sporadically and almost involuntarily. He could see his own tracks from the previous three circuits around the brooding compound. They were already distorted and distended from the warmish south wind, with the still green grass springing back upright after being pressed into the earth. He knew that the snow would soon be gone again, since the forecast called for a warming trend. The wind would then bring the gentle, melting ocean breezes from the Black Sea and the Sea of Azov to the south.

As he walked, the young soldier's thoughts warmed also with restrained hope. This might be the last night that he had to walk around these concrete monstrosities while the bastard *Starshiy Serzhant* slept drunk in the warm control room, basking in the light of the television monitors and perimeter sensors.

From his present vantage point, Bogdanskii could see all of the Golovchino National Nuclear Weapons Storage Facility laid out before him. The site encompassed several square kilometers. Six storage bunkers were dug into the walls of small ravines spread around a circular access road. There was also housing for the officers, utility buildings, a heliport, and the control central, all surrounded by a four-meter-high chain link fence topped with razor wire.

Bogdanskii's route would take him along the inside perimeter of the fence, safely separated from the land mines that were randomly planted along the exterior. Signs in both Russian and Ukrainian warned passersby of their ominous presence. The visitor that he was expecting eventually, however, had no need for the warnings, for he would be with the same men who had planted the mines and had designed their layout.

Bogdanskii briefly reflected on the childish pride that he had initially felt at being conscripted into the twelfth GUMO of the Ministry of Defense to guard Mother Russia's nuclear arsenal, part of which was stored in the concrete tombs before him. Each bunker contained 'special items', almost all of which had been removed from the Ukraine in 1996 following the breakup of the Soviet Union. Now, after months of drudgery, long hours, no pay, and constant hunger gnawing at the base of his spine, he knew better.

Persistent personnel shortages guaranteed that each of Bogdanskii's watches would be at least twelve hours long. The perimeter alarm systems only worked fifty percent of the time, ensuring that he would be outside for the whole watch, taking the place of the automated system.

Even when Bogdanskii was not on duty, he had no place to call home. He had cordoned off a corner of one of the utility buildings with scavenged plastic sheet as his space, and he slept on straw, under a moth-eaten blanket. Had Bogdanskii not been in the army and if he had still lived in his home village of Grayvoron, an ancient site on the Vorskla River a few kilometers to the south, he would have been considered homeless.

Bogdanskii bitterly reflected on the sad state of things. The watches were long and lonely, punctuated only by searches for food in the meager fields surrounding the facility between duty tours for the few potatoes, cabbages, and other vegetables overlooked by the other hungry soldiers. He owed his very existence to the thriving black market that had completely supplanted the local economy, and he also owed the local *fartsovchiks*, the street dealers, debts that he knew he would never be able to repay.

Sometimes, a gray hare or other nocturnal animal would cross Bogdanskii's path on his rounds around the fence perimeter, and he would try to dispatch it without ruining it with his heavy rifle and its 7.62X54-millimeter rounds. He would only occasionally succeed, in the dim light that occupied the tours that were his lot as a junior man.

The facility's officers knew that this extracurricular food gathering went on routinely. They always discretely looked the other way, for they had little enough food for themselves. Also, they could always make up for a few ammunition rounds among those spent in the seemingly ever-ongoing target practice for the soldiers. Sporadic rifle fire was therefore not unusual at any time of the day at the Golovchino facility.

Bogdanskii knew that the officers at the facility did not fare much better than the common soldiers. While the senior men had housing, the houses had no heat and leaky plumbing. Like Bogdanskii, they also were not paid regularly.

Russian currency was effectively worthless at any rate since the dissolution of the Soviet Union. A simple television set cost well over a million rubles, and the smaller denomination, the kopeck, had disappeared completely from circulation

Persistent rumors of hunger strikes and protests had dogged the Golovchino facility for some time. Possible mutiny in the ranks was talked about in hushed tones. Whole families sold their very essence to blood banks to pay for food and for their children's nursery fees. The officers' wives were not even able to take second jobs because of the distance to the nearest town of any size from the facility.

At the thought of the officers' wives, a flush swept across Bogdanskii's face and a warm firmness formed in his groin as he remembered Mariya, his darling *Masha*, his love from secondary school. Her blue eyes, her lips, and the smell of her flaxen hair flooded his senses. He recalled exactly the sight of her budding breasts beneath the filmy blouse in the hazy autumn sunlight set against the wheat field, and the blanket laid down, and the question in her eyes.

Bogdanskii shuddered and cleared his mind. What would his *Masha* think if she saw him sleeping on straw like a farm animal, he wondered? Grayvoron might as well be on the other side of the moon as far as he was concerned; he could never walk the several kilometers there and get back in time for the next tour. And if he did not get back in time he would be shot out of hand, of this he was convinced.

No, his *Masha* must remain only in his memory, Bogdanskii concluded, sadly; cool and enigmatic and forever beautiful, to visit him only in his thoughts on hot, sticky nights upon his bed of straw. But then, he recalled hopefully, the *Polkovnik* had promised that there would be many other *Mashas* for him in his lifetime.

It could have been worse, Bogdanskii considered briefly. He could have been shipped out to one of the many conflicts that the Russian army was currently engaged in: Chechnya, Azerbaijan, Tajikistan, and Turkmenistan, where brother was killing brother. Or, even worse, he could have been like the broken-down, drunken bastard *Starshiy Serzhant* in the control area; a hollow man, with no soul left except what the vodka gave him.

In the few sober moments that Bogdanskii had been able to share with the senior non-commissioned officer, the *Starshiy Serzhant* had told him about the horrors of Afghanistan. He had talked about killing every inhabitant of every village, every old man, woman, child and dog, and then seeding their lands with mini-mines so that no one would ever dare live there again. He had spoken about the special revenge that the Afghan fighters took against captured Soviet soldiers, competing amongst each other for new, innovative ways to kill their captives in the most inhumane ways possible.

The senior man had said that the Afghan women were the worst of all. Many a Russian boy, the sergeant had asserted, had cursed his own mother a thousand times before he was permitted by these women to die. Yes, Bogdanskii thought, it could have been much worse.

Not much longer now, Bogdanskii hoped. Not for him the squalid, peasant life of these *apparatchiks*, content with their meager share of life. His future was assured, the *Polkovnik* had told him. The colonel and his men would enter at the truck gate on a night when he was on duty, Bogdanskii had been told, on a favorable night that would come soon. And all that he had to do was what he always did.

Bogdanskii bent into the south breeze and lit a pungent Russian cigarette, its tobacco black and tarry. He began to walk slowly towards the truck gate, in anticipation of their possible arrival, as the strong plume of smoke encircled his face. Tonight would be a good night for it, he thought.

Bogdanskii knew that the drunken *Starshiy Serzhant* depended on him to wake him before Bogdanskii's last round so that he might appear alert to his relief and to any officer who might occasionally accompany his relief on an early morning tour. The senior man had made this especially clear to Bogdanskii from the very first day of his assignment. The sergeant would occasionally reward him for his diligence with a few smokes from his seemingly endless supply of American cigarettes that he, at least, seemed to be able to afford; cigarettes that were much better than the horseshit that was all that Bogdanskii could get from the *fartsovchiks*. Bogdanskii had idly wondered many times what would happen if he had just let the bastard sleep, but he had no illusions. He knew that the older man would kill him out of hand and that no question would ever be raised. Even in this new Russia, army authority was never questioned.

But, the *Polkovnik* had promised, all of this would change soon. And then it was on to the Crimea, and Bogdanskii would see more beautiful women in a day than lived in all of Grayvoron! At the thought of this wondrous thing, the hot flush swept across his face again and the warm firmness in his groin resumed, and thoughts of Mariya shot in and out of his consciousness.

As he thought of the *Polkovnik*, the tall, spare-framed, blond Russian colonel assumed almost god-like proportions in Bogdanskii's childish mind. A brilliant man, the *Polkovnik*, he thought to himself. And his plan, how elegantly simple! A few 'special items' in the hands of a small, mobile, elite, and highly educated group of soldiers, all committed to the welfare of Mother Russia. They would use the weapons as leverage, and then all of the hunger, all of the injustice and corruption, and all of the *apparatchiks* would be swept away. Russia would become the paradise that had been promised to Bogdanskii for all of his eighteen years.

And how perceptive the man was, Bogdanskii thought admiringly. He had instinctively known that Fyodor Bogdanskii, though only a mere private, was a comrade who could help revive the Socialist vision in this time of imminent crises for the Motherland! Someday, the *Polkovnik* had told him, Bogdanskii's name would be mentioned in the same breath as the old Soviet heroes to Russian secondary school students. Bogdanskii thrilled at the mere thought.

Bogdanskii's chest swelled with pride as he thought of how the *Polkovnik* had shared with him the most intimate details of the plan, proving the depth of his trust of and dependence on the young private. Once they had entered at the truck gate, he had been told, the group would proceed to bunker number 5, where several hundred of the older 'special items' of particular interest to the group, the nuclear artillery shells, were stored, almost haphazardly. Having procured their needs, the group would retrace their steps and await Bogdanskii in the old town of Grayvoron until the end of his shift, leaving everything at the storage site as they had found it.

By morning the snow would have melted, eliminating all traces of the night's visitors. Since the bunkers were seldom entered, and never inventoried, it might be months before the items were found to be missing. By that time, the group would be safely away from Russian authorities in the Crimea, a few *hryvna* having secured their passage across the porous Ukrainian border a few kilometers away. There, the robust Ukrainian underground would guarantee their security while they planned their return to Mother Russia with the 'special items' to liberate her from the dissolute reformists who had perverted her Marxist ideals.

Suddenly, in the quiet night air, Bogdanskii heard the sharp '*clink!*' of metal against metal that announced the visitors' arrival long before the dark figures came into view at the truck gate. He had guessed right; tonight was indeed the night!

Stubbing out his cigarette beneath his boot, the young private quickened his pace and approached the four figures as one of them worked the rusted chain out of the fence gate, its cut link ends bright beneath the yellowish light of the overhead yard lights. Transferring the cut chain to the hand holding the heavy bolt cutter, the stooped figure swung the gate open on its rusted hinges with his free hand to admit the others.

They were all dressed in field camouflage of white, black and brown, almost invisible against the snowy backdrop. All of them carried field packs, side arms, and assault rifles. Bogdanskii saw in the snow that they had walked in each other's tracks through the minefield in a zigzag pattern, easily avoiding the hidden dangers beneath the snow-covered soil, since they knew exactly where each mine had been placed.

Bogdanskii hurriedly approached the lead figure, a tall, spare-framed blond man. The hair of his bare head, free of the camouflage jacket hood that was thrown back casually as if the man was unconcerned, shined like gold beneath the poor lighting.

"So, Comrade Bogdanskii, all is well?" asked the figure, seemingly with detached disinterest and with a small smile playing across his Slavic features. The man's pale blue eyes seemed to dance in his face, and his gaze seemed to burn into Bodanskii's very soul.

"*Da*, Comrade *Polkovnik*", replied Bogdanskii with alacrity. "The bastard *Starshiy Serzhant* is drunk and asleep as usual, and will not expect to be awakened until 0500."

"Now, now, Comrade, you shouldn't judge the *Starshiy Serzhant* so harshly", said the tall blond figure, condescendingly. "The man saw much in Afghanistan. I know," he said with a sigh. "I was there too, and I know what he wants to forget. But he is weak, and therefore he cannot be of any help to us. Enough of this!" he said abruptly. "We have much work to do and there is little time to get it done."

With that, the tall figure bent into a running posture and began to lope across the compound towards a low bunker buried in the wall of a ravine some one hundred meters away. The other camouflaged figures followed him closely, and Bogdanskii brought up the rear, trailing the rest by several meters.

The group brought up short before the doors of the low bunker with Bogdanskii arriving last. The young private was slightly out of breath from the unaccustomed sprint with the heavy Mosin-Nagent bolt-action rifle slung across his shoulder.

The tall leader pointed to the combination lock in the doors' twin hasps, and the man with the bolt cutter attacked it immediately. "I tried to tell them that they needed better locks," said the tall blond *Polkovnik* with a chuckle, to no one in particular, "but no, every kopeck counts, *da*?" His answer was a soft '*clink*', and then another, and then the soft '*thud*' of the heavy brass lock hitting the ground.

As the man with the bolt cutters stepped back, two others each took one of the heavy bay doors and swung them outward, permitting the colonel to enter. He briefly felt along each wall before discovering the switch that turned on the bunker's interior lighting. He switched it on, and the bunker's interior was bathed in a bright white light. It illuminated two fifty-meter long wooden tables, each parallel to the other, running down the entire length of the bunker. Each table was filled side to side with wooden crates, and each crate contained an artillery shell. The grease-covered tip of each shell protruded slightly above the edge of its crate, gleaming dully in the bright light.

Bogdanskii took in the scene with a blink, awestruck. He had never seen the inside of the bunkers that he had guarded for so long. Hundreds and hundreds of shells were contained in this one, in what seemed to him to be two sizes: mostly the standard one hundred fifty-five millimeter round of the Russian Army, but also many of the larger two hundred eight-millimeter round, the largest field artillery in the world.

"*Da*, we Russians, we never throw anything away, do we?" said the tall blond *Polkovnik*, again to no one in particular.

Without further direction from the tall blond colonel, his three companions dispersed to the left-most table and proceeded to the far end of the bunker. The officer followed closely, and upon arriving immediately inspected a group of one hundred fifty-five millimeter shells that rested there in their wooden crates.

After the colonel had pointed out two shell crates, the others, all strapping, heavy-set men, approached the crates and placed two of their field packs on the floor beside them. From each field pack they withdrew a wooden replica of a one hundred fifty-five millimeter artillery shell, covered in a light coating of grease, and set it on the floor. Working together, the three men then withdrew each of the real shells from its crate and placed it inside one of the field packs, replacing each in its crate with one of the wooden replicas. The *Polkovnik* viewed the results with satisfaction. Close enough to pass a cursory inspection, perhaps for months, he thought to himself.

At a command from the tall blond colonel, two of the men squatted before a field pack. Each in turn was assisted by the third in getting the packs' padded straps over his shoulders and the weight-sharing belt secured around his waist. Each then easily lifted his pack and its one hundred pound load in a squat thrust to a standing position.

When both men were standing, the colonel barked another command and the group retreated to the bay doors of the bunker. After the others had closed the heavy bay doors, the colonel secured them with a heavy brass combination lock identical to the one that had been cut for entrance. The group then retraced their steps to the truck entrance, more slowly now with their heavy loads, trying to walk in the footprints of the man in front of him as much as possible.

As the heavily laden soldiers proceeded to the truck entrance, the tall blond *Polkovnik* hung back and slowed his pace until Bogdanskii caught up with him. Throwing his arm around the young private's thin shoulders, he said softly in his ear, "So, Comrade Bogdanskii, do you remember the plan?"

"*Da*, Comrade *Polkovnik*", replied Bogdanskii, excitedly. "After the end of my watch, I am to proceed towards Grayvoron and meet with you and your vehicle two miles from the border, on the road to Kharkiv, at exactly 1000. It is an hour and a half walk, and I should be there with thirty minutes to spare."

"You are a fine young man, and a true patriot," said the tall blond man. Bogdanskii's chest swelled with pride as the colonel quickly placed a liquid-saturated cloth over his mouth and nose and held it there tightly, while grasping his free shoulder without the rifle, for the brief ten seconds that it took for the young private to slip into unconsciousness. The younger man struggled vainly in his arms as he tried to comprehend the *Polkovnik*'s actions.

Releasing his grip on the young man's face, the colonel held the young private's thin body with both arms and almost gently lowered him to the ground, his head lower than his feet on the slight decline. Tenderly, he slipped the heavy Mosin-Nagent bolt-action rifle from the boy's shoulder and jacked a round into the breech. He then placed the muzzle beneath the private's chin and quickly but deliberately pulled the trigger. The young man's body arched with the rifle report as the top of his head was blasted away, and then it twitched spasmodically for a few seconds before becoming still.

After laying the rifle across the boy's chest with one of the young private's gloved fingers inserted into the trigger housing, the colonel rejoined the rest of the group at the truck gate. Then, after replacing the original chain and lock on the gate with an equally rusty replacement, the group struggled with their burdens through the minefield, following the same zigzag steps they had made on the way in, into the darkness of West European Russia. A warm wind was now blowing in from the Sea of Azov, and the snow was melting rapidly.

*   *   *   *

The day shift watch commander of the Golovchino National Nuclear Weapons Storage Facility, accompanied by two soldiers, found young *Ryadovoi* Fyodor Bogdanskii lying on his back, with his rifle upon his chest and with one finger in the trigger housing, in the still-green grass about one hundred meters from bunker number five. It had been only minutes since he had discovered the previous shift *Starshiy Serzhant* asleep at his post. That senior non-commissioned officer was now in detention, and he would be shot the next day.

The watch commander, a veteran Russian soldier of many years experience, looked down on the gray remains of what was left of the young private's sallow face, with all of his hopes and aspirations spread out on the green grass behind him in a yellow-flecked, crimson fan of brains, blood, fatty tissue and bone fragments for a distance of several meters, with detached compassion. The despair of these young conscripts, he knew, was palpable.

Bogdanskii was the fifth such suicide of a young man at the Golovchino National Nuclear Weapons Storage Facility in the past six months, the watch commander thought grimly. God help us, he thought fearfully, if the Germans ever again regain their sense of destiny and look east.

CHAPTER 2

▼

'11/01/01, 2300 hours, course 258 degrees, en route to Devil's Island Light" was the entry that First Officer Burian Klychko had just penned by hand, in Ukrainian, carefully into the worn pages of the ship's log on the bridge of the great ship that was traversing the black, slick waters of Lake Superior. The ship, the *Kharkiv*, a bulk carrier, was presently some twenty miles off the coast of Michigan's Upper Peninsula, east of Ontonagon and north of the abandoned lighthouse referred to on the charts as Fourteen-mile Point. It was owned by the Azov Shipping Company and was based in Mariupol, Ukraine.

Klychko had smiled to himself ruefully as he made the manual entry. Newer commercial ships from other nations had computerized log systems; but such was the state of the economy in the new Ukraine, a nation that had only recently broken away from the grip of the old Soviet Union, that such advances were not possible on an old ship such as the *Kharkiv*.

It was a quiet night, and the Lake Superior surface was a glimmering mirror in the obsidian night, interrupted only where the bow of the ship knifed through it. The blue-over-yellow Ukrainian ensign hung limply by the stern, only occasionally flapping in the atmospheric turbulence caused by the great ship's progress.

Since making the turn to the southwest some five miles off the Eagle Harbor Light after leaving the Soo Locks, the *Kharkiv* had been on what Captain Dovzhenko had called the 'milk run' during the evening meal with the officers: a one hundred twenty mile straight run to the north of Wisconsin's Apostle Islands, to the Devil's Island Light. There the final turn would be made to approach the Duluth Ship Canal.

At 10 knots, it would take the *Kharkiv* about twelve hours to make Devil's Island Light. Captain Dovzhenko had turned the bridge over to First Officer Klychko and had then retired to his quarters for a good night's sleep, to be ready for the navigational challenges of the next day in Duluth harbor.

Even the American pilot, John Smolins, who had boarded the *Kharkiv* as required by U.S. Coast Guard regulations at the head of the St. Mary's River some three miles southeast of Point Iroquois for the run into Duluth, was asleep in an anteroom adjacent to the bridge, to be fresh for the next day's activities. Klychko didn't miss the company of the pilot; he seemed to be an unpleasant man. The pilot seemed to want only to complain about how poorly he was paid, from the little English that Klychko understood, a notion that the Ukrainian found absurd. Smolins spoke no Ukrainian, and conversation with him had been limited to universal navigation terms at any rate.

First Officer Klychko was alone on the bridge, and he relished it. Klychko felt himself to be among the luckiest of men, in charge at the moment of this great ship in the middle of the American Great Lakes and on the greatest lake of them all, Superior. It was the largest freshwater lake in the world, at thirty-one thousand square miles, a figure that made a fair percentage of the total area of his home country, Ukraine.

The *Kharkiv* might be an old ship, Klychko considered, but she still had some strength left to her. Even on the bridge, many meters above the engine room, he could feel her ninety-nine hundred brake horsepower diesel engine throbbing as it twisted the single ten-foot-diameter propeller through the water and pulsed the lifeblood of the ship to where it was needed, to the electrical and mechanical interfaces necessary for commerce and human occupation.

The femininity that Klychko unconsciously assigned to the old ship came naturally to him, for he was a seafaring man. Like innumerable generations of sailors before him, the *Kharkiv* was not simply a ship to Klychko. It was a living thing, and his home. The captain and the crew were his surrogate family, and they were almost his only reason for existing.

The bulk carrier was five hundred eighty-four feet long, with a seventy-five foot beam and a draft of forty-seven feet when fully loaded, with a displacement of twenty-six thousand tons. It had been built in Yokohama, Japan, for the former Soviet Union in the mid-1970's. Three officers and sixteen crew members comprised the ship's compliment, all of whom were cross-trained to do practically everything aboard ship save tearing down the mighty diesel engine that propelled the behemoth.

No modern equipment assisted the navigator or seaman on the *Kharkiv*. The bridge equipment consisted of a rudimentary engine order telegraph, and several antiquated radars, fathometers, and various communications equipment. The cranes and the superstructure on her deck showed rusted components everywhere.

The old girl was beginning to show her age, Klychko knew. The *Kharkiv* now rode high in the water, having discharged her cargo of steel machine and turbine parts at various ports along Lake Huron and Lake Michigan before entering Lake Superior through the Soo Locks. She showed vast swatches of red lead paint below what would normally be her waterline, areas that were now exposed to view since she was running with empty holds. An aging whore, trying to attract young men, was how the crew described her.

But none of that mattered to Klychko at the moment. The ship's disrepair was now invisible in the great darkness of Lake Superior. He could as well have been an ancient mariner sailing into the uncharted waters of the New World on a fine, new ship, so great was his pride.

It had been a difficult voyage. The Americans had become completely, albeit understandably, paranoid following the terrorist attacks on the New York World Trade Center the previous September 11. Even though the *Kharkiv* had already been in the waters of Lake Huron at the time of the attacks, the crewmembers had found themselves treated as potential terrorists at every port of call.

The ship and the crew had been inspected over and over again at each landfall, with every nook and cranny of the ship searched and the crews' personal papers examined rigorously. Facilities at all of their ports of call had prohibited crewmembers from stepping ashore onto facility property, even to make a phone call to their families from the dock; acts which had effectively restricted them to the ship.

It had been even worse on this voyage, Captain Dovzhenko had recalled at the evening meal, than two years previously. Then, another Ukrainian ship, the *Znamia Oktiabria*, also of the Azov Shipping Company, almost had to beg for food from the Ukrainian-American community in New York in order to continue its voyage, due to bureaucratic snafus in the new Ukraine following the dissolution of the Soviet Union. Captain Dovzhenko's brother had been the captain of that vessel. His brother still felt the humiliation very personally, Dovzhenko had confided to the officers at the evening mess.

For his part, Klychko felt extraordinarily lucky to have his assignment as First Officer aboard the *Kharkiv*. First Officer was a major promotion for so young a man as Klychko. It was an assignment that was due in no small part to the close association of his family, who had been seafarers out of Mariupol even during the Nazi occupation of 1941 through 1943 during World War II, with the Dovzhenko family, whose male members had been ship captains as long as anyone could remember. Klychko had shipped with Captain Dovzhenko before, and the older man liked him, he knew.

The Ukrainian fleet was old. Many vessels had been either sold as scrap or to foreign ship owners. Some seventy-five percent of Mariupol sailors languished on shore, unemployed. To have a job, any skilled job, in the new Ukraine was not something to be dismissed lightly, and to be a mariner on a working ship was almost unheard of in these days. Klychko was not ungrateful, and in many respects, he looked upon Captain Dovzhenko as the father he no longer had.

Klychko's real father, a Kiev firefighter, had died a horrible death while responding to the Chernobyl nuclear disaster in 1986, some eighty miles north of Kiev. A testing mistake had created a supercritical reactor condition that had blown the Number 4 reactor's heavy steel and concrete lid off. It had killed many people immediately and up to one hundred thousand people slowly, over the ensuing years, while contaminating much of the earth's northern hemisphere.

After his father's death, he, his mother and his two sisters had fled to Mariupol to his mother's family, who were a family of seafarers. Young Burian had been a bright boy, and all of the family had pitched in to pay his way through Academy, betting on a horse that would sustain them through uncertain times. Now, at the age of twenty-eight, he was the principal support for the entire family, most of whom were unemployed. This was Klychko's first trip aboard the *Kharkiv* to Lake Superior, or to any North American waters on any ship, for that matter.

But at the moment, none of this mattered. Klychko was the temporary master of a great ship, in northern climes. The Northern Lights, that magical interaction of the solar wind with the earth's atmosphere that is only visible at these latitudes, were dancing and shimmering above the invisible dark northern shoreline of Lake Superior. Klychko struggled to pay attention to his duties, for the ship was now on automatic pilot and the view to the north was mesmerizing.

The *Kharkiv* had not been in the Great Lakes for many years, ever since the controversy began in the early 1990's surrounding the introduction of exotic species into the Great Lakes by saltwater vessels. The 'salties' such as the *Kharkiv* had been responsible for the unintentional importation of the zebra mussel, the round goby, the fishhook water flea and the Eurasian ruffe, along with some one hundred seventy-nine other non-native species, through the practice of dumping their ballast tanks upon reaching a lake port.

The invasive species competed for limited aquatic food supplies with the eighteen billon-dollar Great Lakes fishery. They also clogged cooling water intakes with severe economic impacts on many manufacturing and power producing applications, and raised economic hell in general.

American scientists and economists were already seriously proposing that the 'salties' should be banned from using the Welland Canal, despite the almost certain devastation of Midwest industries that rely on foreign goods, such as the steel used by Detroit auto makers. The canal had been built a generation earlier to allow ships to pass around Niagara Falls as they moved from Lake Ontario to Lake Erie.

On this trip, however, ballasting of the *Kharkiv* hadn't been necessary due to the many thousands of tons of steel parts carried as incoming cargo. Having discharged her cargo at several Lake Huron and Lake Michigan ports, the bulk carrier was now on her way to Duluth. There her holds would be cleaned and then reloaded with Minnesota corn bound for western European ports. Although it was late in the shipping season, the economic rewards were more than worth the risk to the owners of the *Kharkiv*. The corn was worth its weight in gold to countries that were struggling with the effects of poor harvests and the rudimentary conversion from collective farming to a capitalist system.

A rap at the door to the bridge broke Klychko's reverie, as he gazed at the kaleidoscopic light show to the north. A swarthy, short-cropped head poked through the door opening and asked, in broken Ukrainian, "Permission to come on the bridge?"

"Come," replied Klychko. It was common for the crew to come to the bridge to take in the sights, for it was the best view on the ship. He had been expecting visitors, once word of the Northern Light display got around the crew quarters. It would be good to share these unique scenes with them.

His visitor entered the bridge and closed the door behind him. Klychko recognized him at once as Taimazov, a Belarusian, the ship's radio operator.

A large, shambling man who resembled a bear, Taimazov was an excellent radio operator. He was also incredibly deft at repairing the few electronic navigational aides carried by the *Kharkiv*. His large fingers were extremely nimble, for a big man, when working with the tiny electronic components and wiring.

Beyond that, Klychko knew little about Taimazov, for the man's Ukrainian was poor. The big man kept mostly to himself, talking little even to the crew men who shared his berth and head. Like most of the crew members assigned to the *Kharkiv*, Taimazov had been provided by a crewing company based in Mariupol, and none of the officers had sailed with him before. To Klychko, however, he seemed to be a solid man, and competent.

"So, Taimazov, have you come to see these magnificent lights?" asked Klychko expansively, sweeping an arm to take in the panorama shimmering to the north as he gazed in that direction.

"Actually, no, First Officer, I have come to order you to stop the ship," replied Taimazov, in his poor Ukrainian. As Klychko's head snapped around in surprise, he found himself looking down the barrel of a nine-millimeter automatic pistol.

"Are you out of your mind, man?" asked Klychko, puzzled but not yet truly afraid. "I can't stop this ship, we have a schedule to keep and you know it."

"First Officer, I do not have time to explain," replied Taimazov flatly. "You will either stop the ship as I have ordered, or I will shoot you and do it myself."

As he looked into Taimazov's cold eyes, Klychko felt fear for the first time. The big man was serious, and he knew it. Frantically, he searched for some logic that he could use to talk him out of this madness.

"Taimazov, you know that the Duluth Coast Guard has us on radar," Kychko said, as he tried to keep his voice calm. "If we stop, they will assume that we are having a problem and they will investigate immediately."

"Actually, First Officer, I have already advised the Coast Guard that we are going to be lying to for a few hours at our present position, to refresh the crew and to be able to enter the grain docks during daylight hours for the convenience of all concerned. No one will be coming. You now have five seconds to ring up 'Stop', or you are a dead man," replied Taimazov, calmly.

Klychko briefly and ludicrously reflected on the fact that the man's Ukrainian had suddenly become much better before abruptly coming to his senses. He then dove for the engine order telegraph and moved the brass lever to 'STOP'.

Taken by surprise, it took the engine room watch a full twenty seconds to return the 'STOP' command and to begin to slow the big diesel engine.

As the great propeller slowed and the familiar engine reverberations lessened, Captain Dovzhenko burst through the door to the bridge in his underwear almost immediately, in confusion and interrupted sleep.

"Klychko, what is wrong?" the Captain asked worriedly, as his eyes swept the bridge searching for the source of the problem. As his gaze fell upon his radio operator leveling an automatic pistol at him, Dovzhenko understood immediately.

"Sorry to disturb you, Captain," said Taimazov, flatly. "Would you please order the deckhands to deploy the boarding ladder on your port side after the ship has lost headway? You will be receiving visitors shortly."

The door to the bridge burst open and the American pilot, John Smolins, barged onto the bridge, half dressed. "What the fuck is going on?" he yelled at the top of his voice. "Don't you commie bastards know that you can't stop a ship in the shipping lane? You ignorant...."

Smolins' tirade was cut short by the loud report of the pistol in Taimazov's hand. A third round, red eye, directly between his other two eyes, briefly appeared on Smolins' face, along with a look of amazement, before he pitched face down on the floor of the bridge, with his hands and feet twitching spasmodically and the back of his head blown away.

Ignoring the corpse on the floor, Taimzov addressed the Captain and his First Officer: "I will tolerate no more interference or delay of my orders. Now please make ready to receive your visitors," he said calmly, in his now excellent Ukrainian.

They all heard the craft before they saw it, heard the low growl of its four-stroke outboard engines far across the calm waters. And about fifteen minutes after the *Kharkiv* had come to a complete stop, they saw a twenty-foot inflatable Zodiac, powered by twin one hundred twenty-five horsepower Yamaha outboards. The craft was running without lights, approaching the boarding ladder from the south. Then, after securing the Zodiac to the base of the boarding ladder, three figures clad in black scrambled up the ladder, one after the other, each carrying what looked to be an assault weapon with a skeleton stock slung across his back.

After reaching the main deck, the lead figure, a tall, spare-framed blond man, with his black jacket hood flung back as if unconcerned about showing himself, made his way the several flights of stairs to the bridge. Entering the bridge area, the blond man nodded to Taimazov, who nodded back in obvious deference. He then walked directly to Captain Dovzhenko and addressed him: "Good evening, Captain," he said lightly. "I am sorry to disturb your voyage, but it will not be for too long. My name is Gregor."

"Gregor? Is that your real name?" asked the Captain, apprehensively.

"Of course not," said the blond man, with some amusement, "but it will serve for our business here tonight. You have some things that belong to us, and we have come to collect them."

"Something that belongs to you?" asked Captain Dovzhenko, incredulously. "Impossible, we have nothing, our holds are empty."

"Oh, you most certainly have them," said the blond man with a chuckle. "The ship has been carrying them for us since its overhaul at the Azov Shipyard this past winter. However", he said, condescendingly, "we never intended that you would find them."

"What could we possibly have that you would want?" Captain Dovzhenko pressed.

"This is not your concern," replied the blond man, suddenly business-like. Motioning to Smolin's corpse, he went on: "As you can see from my colleague's work, we are serious men. Now please, Captain, have your men assemble in the crew's lounge so that we may tell you of our needs. I shouldn't need to tell you what will happen if any further interference is attempted," he concluded, ominously

After ordering all of the crew to the crew's lounge over the ship's public address system, the Captain and his First Officer were escorted to it by Taimazov and the tall blond man. When all nineteen crewmembers had been accounted for, the blond man addressed them while Taimazov and the other black-clad figures stood by, with weapons at the ready.

"Gentlemen and lady," the blond man said, giving a quick nod to the ship's cook, who was the only female on board, "we are sorry to interrupt your voyage, but we have come to collect some things that belong to us. If we receive a minimum of cooperation, we shall have them and be gone, leaving you free to resume your journey in an hour's time. Now," he continued briskly, "we shall require the assistance of the deckhands and the ship's welder," he said, as his eyes swept the assembly.

Four men stood. They were escorted out of the lounge by two of the black clad figures who had been standing by and by the tall blond man who had called himself Gregor.

Once the others had left, the door to the crew's lounge was closed. The rest of the crew, the Captain and First Officer included, remained behind. Taimazov, who had exchanged his automatic pistol for an assault weapon, guarded them. First Officer Klychko had noted with considerable trepidation that none of the black-clad figures had made any attempt to disguise his features.

Considerable discussion ensued among those who remained about what the strangers could possibly be after. Drugs, said one, opium from Afghanistan for the American heroin market. Precious metals or stones, said another, to avoid import tariffs. Taimazov made no attempt to discourage the discussion, as if knowing that by having something to talk about, the crewmembers became easier to guard.

On the main deck, the deckhands had been directed to remove the most forward of two hatch covers on the number four hold that was immediately in front of the bridge and the crew accommodations block, using the adjacent forty-ton crane. Once the hatch cover had been removed, the ship's welder, a portable acetylene welding machine, the welder's gear, and one of the black-clad figures were lowered into the hold in a personnel carrier.

Upon reaching the bottom of the hold, the welder was set to work cutting a five foot wide by five foot high square into the lower left-hand corner of the bulkhead that separated the number four hold from the next forward number three hold, along chalk lines drawn by the black clad figure. The acetylene torch made quick work of the quarter-inch plate steel that comprised the bulkhead. In thirty minutes, the severed plate fell out of the bulkhead onto the floor of the hold with a loud '*clang*', revealing two wooden crates on wooden racks, surrounded by fiberglass insulation.

Each of the crates, both fairly heavy, was removed from its rack by the two men, with some effort, and then was hoisted, using the crane and the personnel carrier, to the main deck. After the crates had been removed, the ship's welder and his escort were retrieved from the hold, leaving the welding equipment behind.

Two of the black-clad figures then climbed down the boarding ladder to the Zodiac. One of the crates was then lowered to the Zodiac by the deckhands and was secured in the center of the craft using tie-downs by the two men below. When this had been accomplished, leaving one crate still on the main deck, the tall blond man then escorted the four *Kharkiv* crewmen back to the crew's lounge to rejoin their mates.

The tall blond man who called himself Gregor then again addressed them: "Gentlemen, and lady," he said, again nodding briefly to the female ship's cook, with the faintest of smiles playing across his features, "I would like to thank you for your cooperation. We shall now leave and bother you no more. We ask only that you remain here for thirty minutes so that we may get underway without interference. Captain," he said grandly, addressing Dovzhenko, "I give you back your ship." And with that, the blond man, accompanied by Taimazov, left the crew's lounge, closing the door behind them.

The buzz began immediately after the exit of the strangers. They had left one of the crates behind, what could it be? Was it a reward for their cooperation, a sharing of their loot? The Captain and his First Officer spoke privately together, in hushed tones, that it was likely something far more ominous than that.

The crewmembers continued their excited chattering for thirty minutes until the first man brave enough to try the door found it chained shut. There was no way out. The crew's lounge was only a metal box, albeit comfortably decorated in paneling and furniture; they would have to claw their way out of it with their fingernails unless help arrived soon. All of them were now pensive, and afraid. They thought of their loved ones, and they prayed to whatever gods they had.

*   *   *   *

At the mouth of the Firesteel River, where that modest stream deposits its contents into Lake Superior some five miles northwest of the village of Ontonagon, the old man sat on a lawn chair, on the beach, wrapped in a sleeping bag. He was staring to the west, as he always did on this particular night in November: the first day of the month of *guckudin*, as it was expressed in the old *Anishinabe* language, 'when it freezes'.

The old man was staring at *Ke-che-gum-me*, the Great Water of his ancestors; a sacred place, protected by *Nanabijou*, the Spirit of the Deep Water. The Northern Lights danced in extravagant display along the northern shore of the Big Lake, but the old man paid them no mind, for his focus was elsewhere.

The old man had been coming to this place each year from his home in Baraga on this day for seventy years, ever since he had been old enough to drive, always looking for the *Megis*, the 'seashell' of Ojibwa legend. He was far too old to drive now, but his grandson had humored him today and had driven him to this place, even though he was far too modern a young Ojibwa man to believe in the old legends anymore.

The old man imagined that his grandson would be well into a pint of whiskey by now. He would be sitting in the car parked by the side of the county road by the bridge that crossed the Firesteel, with its heater on. The young man would be wishing that he was somewhere else, but he did not want to offend his grandfather, whom he seemed to sense had a sort of mystical connection with this place.

For his part, the old man sat quietly, recalling the old legends that had been handed down from his ancestors. He often regretted that he and his sons had been so remiss, so focused on improving the material lot of their people, while neglecting to teach the young ones about where they had come from.

He again remembered what his own father had told him, over and over, until he had known it by heart. "When our grandfathers lived on the great salt water," his father had chanted, "the great *Megis*, the seashell, showed above the surface of the water to reflect the sun and warm the *An-ish-in-aub-ag*, the red race. But then it sank into the waters, and our grandfathers were left in darkness and despair."

"But when the people had reached the great river that drains the big lakes at *Mo-ne-aung*," he had continued, "where the Montreal of the white man now stands, the *Megis* rose again to give life and reflect back the rays of the sun. For a long time it warmed our grandfathers. But then it sank, until the people had reached the first big lake that is now called Lake Huron, when it rose again to show them its shining face."

"But again it sank," the chant had continued, "and death lived among the wigwams of the people, until they had reached *Bow-e-ting*, that the white man calls Sault Ste. Marie today. Then the *Megis* rose again, to warm them and give them light. Now it remained for a long time. But, at last it disappeared again, bringing misery and darkness."

"Now," his father had chanted, "the people divided themselves to seek the light again. They became the people of the Three Fires: the Ojibwa, the Ottawa, and the Pottawatumies."

"As they traveled westward along the north and south shores of *Ke-che-gum-me*," the chant went on, "your grandfathers of the Ojibwa did not see the *Megis* again until it once more rose, when the people had at last come to *Mon-ing-wun-a-kaun-ing*, the place of the gold-breasted wood-pecker," referring to Madeline Island in the Apostle archipelago of western Lake Superior. "And here the great *Megis* rose again, and it shined for a very long time."

"At *Mon-ing-wun-a-kaun-ing* the Ojibwa people grew like a great tree," chanted his father, "and spread their branches in all directions, and their old men lived out the full measures of their lives. This is the meaning of the seashell," he had added, pointedly, "for it represents the great *Megis*."

"My son," his father had told him, "the great *Megis* has again sunk beneath the surface of the great water, and our people again live in igno-rance and misery. You must always look to *Mon-ing-wun-a-kaun-ing*, the place of the gold-breasted woodpecker and the gathering place of your grandfathers, for here last the great *Megis* shown upon them before it sank into the waters. You must look west down *Ke-che-gum-me*, each first night of the *guckudin*, until at last the great *Megis* shines again. And then," he had concluded, "the Eighth Fire will begin, and a young warrior will arise to lead our people west to greatness."

The old man had thereafter faithfully adhered to his father's command, even as he had spent a lifetime trying to improve the material lot of the *Anishinabe* at Baraga. He was here again tonight, as he always was on this date.

The place that he now occupied, at the mouth of the Firesteel River, had another more subtle and much more ironic meaning for the old man. It was the closest drivable point to a place only a few miles to the northeast, a place adjacent to the abandoned Fourteen-Mile Point lighthouse. It was a parcel of land originally of almost twenty-six hundred acres that had been ceded to thirty-six members of the Ontonagon band of Ojibwa Indians during the great Federal land grab of the 1850's. It was still shown on many maps as the 'Ontonagon Indian Reservation'.

Bracketing the West Sleeping River at its mouth at Sleeping Bay in Lake Superior, the parcel had never been occupied by the Ojibwa, for the land was poor and access was remote. To the old man's knowledge, the place had only been occupied by one person ever since that time, a lone trapper who probably wasn't even Ojibwa.

The 'reservation' had dwindled since the time of its creation to a mere 300 acres or so at present, as those Ojibwa who could prove their claims had sold it off. But still, it always amused the old man to think of it: a classic example of the white man's generosity towards his red brother, who had originally occupied the entire Upper Peninsula in the first place.

Wah, wah, wah, thought the old man; another year gone by. He did not have many more left, and still the *Megis* had not come.

The old man had noticed, absently, the freighter's running lights on the horizon to the west, and he now became slowly aware that they had not changed position in some time. He had also heard the low roar of the outboards proceeding to the south about an hour previously, although he had not given them much thought at the time. Some late season fisherman, he had assumed, taking advantage of the rare, silky-quiet Lake Superior night, and probably taking out at the end of the Four-Mile Rock Road just northeast of Ontonagon.

And then, suddenly, the old man saw it—the Great *Megis*, growing slowly, rising out of the waters due west like an enormous seashell. A red cloud, in a mushroom shape, reached for the black sky, with fingers of fire streaking from it in all directions. It is true, the old man thought excitedly, it is all true! It is the Eighth Fire! We will be delivered and....

The old man's thought was abruptly interrupted as his eyes were cauterized by the blast, milliseconds before his withered body was vaporized and was spewed into the trees behind him. The trees were then blown into a giant pile of pick-up-sticks for hundreds of yards in both directions along the shoreline. The entire jumbled mass of wreckage steamed and smoked, and which part of it was the old man's soul, rejoining his ancestors, could not be discerned.

*   *   *   *

Some fifty miles to the south, another man clung halfway up a thirty-seven meter high manmade tower over a quarter-mile above sea level, transfixed by the dancing Northern Lights. The man was a physicist, and he well understood the science of the interplay between solar flares and their iridescent interaction with the Earth's northern atmosphere. But, at times like these he always thought to himself that science gave way to true art, God's art, written large on the vast velvet pallet of the northern sky.

Even in the black night, illuminated only by the shimmering display to the north, the man's hands and face seemed to glow, so white were they, as he gripped the steel frame of the tower. His transparent flaxen hair was covered by a watch cap pulled down low over his ears. He took in the display to the north with eyes the irises of which were colorless and which appeared in normal light to be a pale blue. Ruefully, he thought that although his condition had made him legally blind, it had at least done so to the extent of far-sightedness, the better to view this grand display.

Only at night did the man dare to take his almost daily exercise, a vigorous hike among the stark, leafless trees and rugged, hilly terrain of this country. His eyes were hypersensitive to light; without any of the natural pigment melanin in his skin, exposure to sunlight was for him a death sentence, a slow, painful death from skin cancer.

'Oculocutaneous albinism', the doctors had told his parents many years previously in his home country of Ukraine; a genetic disorder that had made him an outcast, a 'freak show', as even he referred to himself. He still recalled the cruel taunts of his classmates at school, the stares and the whispered 'Ghost Boy' and 'Maggot' asides.

The pale man had suffered complete social stigmatization and isolation, until the state had recognized his gifts and had taken him from his parents. After that, he had been tutored and academically developed in a special environment that was designed to meet his physical needs. And so had he matured. Over time, he had developed into one of the most brilliant physicists of the age, completely alone and in darkened places, a man unable to bear the sight of the sun.

But, even then, he had never been truly alone. There had always been the 'keepers', even before he had been brought to this new place, always there to attend him and to provide for his physical, equipment, and academic needs. And so it was here; he had only to make a request, and whatever was needed appeared, as if by magic.

And even now, here on this tower, he was not alone, he knew. The new keeper, the Indian, would be there below him at the base of the tower as he always was, as if to give him some space. The Indian was ever-present, no matter how far he might travel in a night's time, before the impending dawn sent him scurrying back to his comfortable hole in the ground, to briefly rest and refresh before again grappling with his momentous experiments with gravity.

As the pale man continued to take in the ghostly panorama being played out in the sky before him, a brief but intense flash of light from behind the backdrop of the high ground to the north caused him to momentarily wince in pain as the dull flash impacted his unprotected eyes. The flash was followed by a low, lingering concussion several seconds later, as if caused by far-away thunder. That was not natural, the physicist thought to himself; it was an explosion of some sort, he was sure of it.

The scientist had no idea of what lay behind the high ground to the north. All he knew of his surroundings was the ground that he had managed to explore since he had been brought here. No maps or discussion of local terrain had ever been provided to him, and so socially traumatized was he that he had never thought to ask, for his work was his entire world.

The physicist knew that it would do no good to ask the Indian about the cause of the flash. They spoke different languages, and the Indian seldom spoke in any event. He usually kept some distance from the pale man as if he was somehow fearful or in awe of him, a reaction that was all too familiar to the scientist. The pale man would have been astonished to know how accurate his casual assessment of the Indian was.

At the base of the tower, Agent Thomas Loonsfoot of the United States Central Intelligence Agency also observed the blast to the north with some alarm. It's a long way from here, he thought to himself, past the Trapp Hills, maybe all the way to Ontonagon.

But what in Ontonagon could make an explosion that big, Loonsfoot asked himself, drawing on his Army Special Operations background. There wasn't anything up there but a small paper mill that he was aware of. This was more like something on the order of a big refinery, or even bigger, going up. As if guarding old *Nanabozho* here wasn't spooky enough, he thought to himself with some trepidation, glancing towards the pale man automatically. Well, he would find out soon enough, as soon as they were back in the bunker.

Loonsfoot was thirty years old, and he had been a CIA agent ever since his Army discharge seven years previously. Born and raised in the nearby town of Watersmeet, Loonsfoot was a full-blooded Ojibwa, a member of the Lac Vieux Desert Band. He had hunted and fished in the surrounding area for most of his life. When the Agency had needed someone to monitor the activities of the pale Ukrainian physicist that they had relocated to a secret underground complex in the Sylvania Wilderness of the Ottawa National Forest, he had been the obvious choice.

For the past three months, Loonsfoot had monitored every waking activity of the scientist, except for some time every few weeks when the man was deeply engrossed in some phase of his research that would permit him to be locked down. At these times, Loonsfoot would be briefly relieved by another agent, which allowed him to go to Watersmeet to visit family and friends.

No one in the tribe really knew what Loonsfoot did, except that he worked for the government, and that was sufficient explanation for his brief visits. Men of the *Anishinabe* felt no need to explain their comings and goings to anyone, nor were any explanations expected from them.

Loonsfoot had heard in the town of Watersmeet and at the Lac Vieux Desert Casino about the rumors going around the tribe. Occasionally, the rumors said, *Nanabozho*, the Great Rabbit, the trickster of Ojibwa legend, would be seen in the woods south of U.S. Highway 2, by old men on nighttime hunting and fishing expeditions or by young men cruising on the two-tracks in cars, with girls and a case of Bud Light.

Loonsfoot had always carefully declined to comment on the rumors. He was well aware that passersby had spotted the man in his charge, while on his almost nightly hikes, on several occasions. It was best for all, he thought, if the tribe chose to believe the rumors. Among the Ojibwa, his charge would then be considered to be sacred, as were all of the old Ojibwa spirits. The whole tribe would unconsciously help him protect the man and his privacy by maintaining their silence to outsiders, if nothing else.

Loonsfoot was a thoroughly modern man, Agency-educated and objective. But, whenever he watched the pale man from his vantage point in the trees or from the base of the tower, or while he watched him at work among his scientific apparatus with his usually dormant Ojibwa spiritual senses tingling, Loonsfoot was sometimes not completely convinced that he didn't believe the *Nanabozho* rumors himself.

After a few moments, when the disturbance to the north had died away, the pale scientist left his perch on the tower without being bidden and began to climb down. Dawn would be breaking in an hour or so, and it was time for both of them to get back to the bunker. There they would be swallowed up by the earth, to avoid the damning sunlight like some transplanted Transylvanian nightmare and his Indian caretaker in the western Upper Peninsula of Michigan.

CHAPTER 3

▼

One a.m., and I'm going through my nightly ritual: sitting back in my Lazy Boy in my bathrobe, staring holes in the ceiling and wrestling with my demons, thought Sidney Hornberg, ruefully. Hornberg was the Resident Agent-in-Charge of the Federal Bureau of Investigation in Marquette, Michigan, and his career was at a dead end, he was sure of it.

Sleep would not come easily for him this night; it never did, anymore. Even the sleeping pill and the couple of belts from the bottle of 'Old Overshoes' in the cupboard wouldn't help tonight, he knew from long experience. No, he would sit here, with his mind spinning like a wheel propelled by some frenzied gerbil, until sheer exhaustion claimed him hours later. Then he would be able to rejoin his wife in their upstairs bedroom for a brief couple hours sleep before the next day's madness began again.

I am exactly fifty-four and a half years old today, Hornberg reflected gloomily, in the early morning hours of November 2, 2001. I should be looking forward to my golden and well-deserved retirement in a few months, his inner voice said. But no, here I am, feeling like I'm going to stroke out before then. Hornberg felt his heart briefly go into arrhythmic palpitations. This was happening more and more frequently now, and it worried him.

9/11 had changed everything for Sidney Hornberg. Before then, his assignment in Marquette had been an ideal assignment for an older agent: usually dull, always predictable, and generally comfortable. But since 9/11, the mostly unguarded U.S.-Canadian border, always vaguely worrisome, had taken on a new importance to Federal law enforcement. It was if government strategic thinkers had just suddenly become aware of the existence the Great Lakes-St. Lawrence Seaway System.

The Seaway was twenty-three hundred miles long, and it permitted uninterrupted navigation for nine months of the year to eight U.S. states and two Canadian provinces, from the Atlantic Ocean to the western extremity of the Great Lakes at Duluth, Minnesota. It was also a system that Hornberg's Marquette FBI office sat squarely astride of. Two hundred million tons of cargo moved through the system each year.

The region served by the system was the home of approximately one hundred million people, or roughly a third of the combined U.S.-Canadian population. Twenty-five U.S. cities of over one hundred thousand residents were located within a hundred miles of a Great Lakes port.

Hornberg now found that his Marquette FBI office was being constantly deluged with demands on it that he and his small staff could not possibly comply with. His hapless attempts to sort out the various competing priorities and local needs for the Bureau had invariably left someone in an official position with his Federal nose out of joint.

All vessels, both foreign-flagged and U.S.-flagged, were being scrutinized as never before, and all merchant mariners in general were being regarded as potential terrorists. Hornberg was also privately convinced that the new Department of Homeland Security that loomed on the horizon, as surely as the sun that would soon be coming up, wasn't going to make his job any easier, either; another layer of bureaucracy to wade through every day, he thought glumly.

Finally, after another hour of mentally juggling the same thoughts over and over again, Hornberg felt himself nod off for a second; the sleeping pill was kicking in at last. As he pushed himself out of the Lazy Boy to rejoin his wife in their upstairs bedroom, he absently noted a loud '*CLAP*' of noise somewhere to the west. Kind of late in the year for a thunderstorm, he thought sleepily, as he made his way up the stairs. Well, what the hell, he reasoned, it might as well thunderstorm in November, everything else in the world is upside down.

*   *   *   *

The phone on the bed stand on Hornberg's side of the bed jangled loudly. Hornberg awoke and grabbed it quickly, as his wife moaned lowly in her sleep with her back to him. He glanced quickly at the alarm clock: 0433. Putting the receiver to his ear, he answered, thickly, "Hornberg residence."

"Sid, Paul Adams here," the mechanical voice in the earpiece replied. Adams was the Michigan State Police Detective stationed in Houghton. "I thought that you'd want to hear this from me before you got to your office today," Adams continued quickly. "Somebody just set off a nuke on Lake Superior."

Hornberg blinked in disbelief. After a moment, he said, in confusion, "I'm sorry, Paul, but I thought you just said that somebody set off a nuke on Lake Superior."

"You heard me right," said Adams, stonily. "About fifteen miles northeast of Ontonagon, out in the lake."

After another few moments of silence, Hornberg asked, shrilly, "A *nuke*? Paul, are you sure?"

"Pretty damn sure," Adams responded grimly. "The Coast Guard at Duluth was watching a Ukrainian freighter dead in the water at that spot when their radar got fried, so they sent a plane out to take a look. Poof, no more freighter. Also, the only radiation instrument the plane had on board pegged. Lots of damage on the Ontonagon County shoreline below Fourteen-mile Point too, I hear from the local cops."

"Casualties?" asked Hornberg.

"Probably, don't know yet," replied Adams, matter-of-factly. "We're scrambling right now to come up with anti-contamination clothing, meters and stuff to get in and take a closer look. Doesn't sound like Ontonagon village got it too bad, though. The sheriff there says that a couple of trees got knocked down east of town, and that's about it. We'll know more in a couple hours."

The phone was silent in Hornberg's hand for several seconds. Then, Hornberg said, slowly, "Jeez, Paul, the shit is really going to hit the fan now."

"Yeah, buckle your chinstrap, bucky, it's going to be a rough ride," replied Adams with mock humor. "Hell, you might as well get up and go to work, Sid, you won't be sleeping any more tonight anyway."

*   *   *   *

The briefing, held in the Michigan State Police headquarters in Houghton that morning at 10 a.m., was conducted in tight secrecy. Present were officials of the state and Ontonagon and Houghton County governments; the Coast Guard Commander at Duluth; a four star Army General stationed at the Pentagon unlucky enough to have been vacationing in the area; Hornberg and Adams; and several physicists from the faculty at Michigan Technological University in Houghton. The media, which was not present, had been told only that a strong explosion had occurred on a foreign-flagged vessel off the Ontonagon County coast, most likely caused by fumes from an improperly vented hold.

The Coast Guard Commander began his briefing. "Ladies and gentlemen, what we are about to tell you must not leave this room. We cannot afford a public panic," he cautioned.

"At approximately 0330 Eastern Standard Time today," the speaker continued, in a flat tone, "we have strong evidence that a low-yield nuclear device was detonated aboard a Ukrainian-flagged vessel, the *Kharkiv*. Before the explosion, the ship was dead in the water, some fifteen miles northeast of the village of Ontonagon, at latitude forty-six degrees, fifty-five minutes, forty-seven seconds north and longitude eighty-nine degrees, fourteen minutes, twenty-nine seconds west," the senior officer said, referring to notes before him.

"Coast Guard divers have confirmed that the *Kharkiv* is sunk at that position in several separate sections, in two hundred feet of water," he continued, grimly. "Her crew of nineteen and one United States merchant vessel pilot is presumed to be lost. Their identities are presently being withheld pending notification of next of kin." With this, the assembled officials looked about the room in stunned silence.

"At the moment there also appears to be at least one casualty on shore," the Commander continued. "This person's identity is unknown at this point." The crumpled vehicle with the Ojibwa Nation license plate that he was referring to had been quickly discovered by the rescue teams at the Firesteel River bridge. It would take dental records, and probably a DNA analysis of the gelatinous mass inside of what was left of the vehicle, to identify the victim, and then only if the remains could be decontaminated.

"There is some radioactive contamination of the shoreline," the Commander continued, matter-of-factly, "but it appears to mostly be confined to the area south of Fourteen-Mile Point, and cleanup efforts are underway." Already, several hundred pounds of debris sat in the area in yellow-and-magenta plastic bags. Urgent pleas had gone out to the closest nuclear plants for more bags, containers, and radiation protection personnel.

"The affected areas have been cordoned off," said the Commander, referring to the four square miles of shoreline known so far to be contaminated. He now addressed the officials sternly: "Gentlemen and women, your cooperation in your various capacities to prevent access by the public to these areas is critical. We must prevent additional injuries and the additional spread of contamination."

"That concludes the formal presentation," stated the Commander. "I'll now throw it open to such questions as we can answer this early in the investigation. Please be advised, however, that any answer we may give is only our best guess at this point."

A hand shot up. A local sheriff asked, "Just how big was this bomb, anyway?"

The commander deferred to one of the physicists. "Well," said the man, hesitantly, "we can only speculate that it was a bomb at this point. But, just based strictly on the damage that we see, it would appear that it had a yield on the order of one hundred to two hundred tons of TNT. To put that number in perspective," he continued, flatly, "that is about a hundredth of the size of the bomb dropped on Hiroshima."

"Do they make atomic bombs that small?" the sheriff asked as a follow-up question, with a puzzled expression on his face.

The Coast Guard Commander briefly conferred with the Army General, and he then responded, carefully, "Unfortunately, yes. Torpedoes, surface-to-surface and air-defense missiles, anti-submarine weapons, ground mines, and artillery shells can all employ low-yield warheads of this size, and even smaller."

A silence now enveloped the room. After several seconds, another hand shot up. A different local official asked, "Is Lake Superior now radioactively contaminated?"

The physicist conferred with his colleagues for a few moments, and then he responded quietly, "Well, yes, the immediate waters surrounding the wreck are certainly heavily contaminated at the moment. The divers who were sent down to verify the location of the *Kharkiv* required extensive decontamination." The local officials looked at each other in dismay.

"But you have to remember," the physicist continued, "Lake Superior is the largest of the Great Lakes and holds more water than any other lake in the world, with the single exception of Lake Baykal in Siberia, which is a deeper lake even than Superior. The radioactive contamination introduced by this explosion," he explained, "is going to eventually be diluted many millions of times, and at some point it will almost certainly reach a safe level. The commercial nuclear industry has a saying," he added, lightly: "'The Solution to Pollution is Dilution'!" A nervous chuckle ran through the audience of officials.

"At the same time, however," the physicist continued, more seriously, "you all need to consider the implications for your municipal water supplies. Remember, the flushing time of Lake Superior—that is, the time it takes for all of the water now in the lake to be replaced by new water—is almost two hundred years. That means", he added quietly, "that the radioactive contamination introduced by this explosion is still going to be in the lake two hundred years from now."

The audience fell silent as they struggled to grasp the implications of this new information. The briefing was over.

*   *   *   *

The car ride back to Marquette from Houghton had been a regular Chinese fire drill, Hornberg thought bleakly. His cell phone had rung incessantly. The President wanted answers "right NOW," he'd been told by his superiors in Detroit. The Ukrainian Ambassador in Washington was apoplectic, said someone else, and the Russians were howling mad, said another. The media wouldn't be put off forever, said still another; already the D.C. press corps smelled a skunk. It had finally gotten to the point where Hornberg had simply turned off his cell phone in order to concentrate on his driving, knowing what must be waiting for him at his Marquette office.

If there was a silver lining to any of this, Hornberg thought ironically, it was that there was no way the FBI was going to let a fifty-four and a half-year-old, burned out field agent in Marquette take the ball. No way at all; the Director himself would be up to his elbows in this one, along with the CIA, the NSC, the State Department, and the Pentagon. Not that they wouldn't make his life a living hell in the meanwhile, but he was going to have all of the help on this one that he could possibly stand.

Upon arriving at his office on West Ridge in Marquette Township, Hornberg was handed a stack of messages by his secretary from people whom he was expected to contact immediately. He thumbed through the stack quickly: FBI and police officials, several congressmen, the Michigan governor, and assorted self-important dignitaries. One message, however, stood out. It said, simply: "1300 tomorrow. Your office. Gregor."

*   *   *   *

The next afternoon, Hornberg's small office in the Marquette FBI building was packed with as many officials of the different state and Federal agencies as could reasonably be crammed into it. The overflow spilled out of the office and down the hall. His desk phone had been connected to a speaker receiver, which fed other speakers located at strategic locations throughout the building. Other leads from the phone went to two laptop computers in the hall, at desks manned by an expert from NASA on Global Positioning System satellite technology and another manned by a representative from the local telephone company.

At precisely 1300, the phone on Hornberg's desk rang. He let it ring exactly two times, and then he answered. "Hornberg," he said flatly into the speaker receiver.

"Good afternoon, Mr. Hornberg, I am Gregor," said the disembodied voice that was being broadcast throughout the building.

"Gregor. Do I know you?" Hornberg asked the ethereal voice, ingenuously.

A quiet chuckle replied to his question. "No, Mr. Hornberg, you do not know me, at least not yet. But I do know you. I know where you live, and I know who your wife is, and I know all of your immediate family on both sides and where they live. I even know," the voice continued, dispassionately, "of that time in Baltimore, long ago, when you cut out the throat of that Palestinian swine with your pocket knife."

Hornberg froze as the remembered image played back in his memory. Only a handful of people in the Bureau knew of that time when, as a young FBI agent, he and another agent had stumbled across three armed PLO members in a warehouse on the Baltimore waterfront, with their crates of arms and explosives ready to be shipped to Palestine. It had never been made known outside the Bureau.

"How is it that you know so much about me, Gregor?" Hornberg asked, curiously, into the ether.

"Come, come, you are being too modest, Mr. Hornberg," replied the voice, merrily. "You were quite famous for that little episode in my former line of work."

Hornberg glanced quickly at the desk manned by the telephone company representative. The man shook his head, in futility. 'Gregor' was obviously using a cell phone. It was all up to the NASA people now.

"And what line of work was that, Gregor?" Hornberg asked politely.

"Another time, Mr. Hornberg, another time," replied the voice, mechanically. "I know that you are trying to pinpoint my present location using your GPS satellite technology. Suffice it for now," the voice continued coldly, "to know that I am responsible for that explosion you witnessed over your big lake yesterday. Goodbye, we shall talk again soon." And then the connection went dead.

"Bingo, got him!" cried the NASA man at one of the tables with the laptops. He briefly poured over a map provided by a Michigan State Police sergeant at his side, and then he shouted, "Christ! That sonofabitch is right here in Marquette in the Wal-Mart parking lot!"

The many faces in the room looked at each other briefly in shocked amazement, and then the entire assembly made a mad dash out of the room, shouting orders as they ran. In less than a minute, thirty City of Marquette and state police cars were screaming down U.S. Highway 41 to the location of the big Supercenter, where they set up roadblocks on all of the exits and entrances.

When all of the police were in place, a heavily armed Michigan State Police SWAT unit rushed the big parking lot, terrifying several hundred shoppers who were leaving the lot or who were returning to their vehicles. They searched all of the people and all of the many cars in the lot and on the roadways thoroughly. But all that was found was an unclaimed cell phone, lying on top of the base stanchion of one of the many outdoor lights that illuminated the parking lot after dark at the twenty-four hour a day business.

CHAPTER 4

▼

"Goddammit, Sam, you crazy sonofabitch!" shouted Bill McCombs in complete frustration, as the springer spaniel tore off in hot pursuit of the doe and her fawn. McCombs was standing in the creek bottom that ran out of Bob Lake in the Ottawa National Forest, about half way between Mass City and Kenton. It was his own fault, McCombs reflected ruefully, for never having trained the dog properly, as he watched the dog in its hunter-orange vest, with its ears flopping and its legs a blur, in pursuit of its quarry like some neon hound from hell.

McCombs knew from long experience that the spaniel would pull up after several hundred yards and end the game. The dog never let McCombs get out of its sight, for fear of missing out on something else that might be amusing on their almost daily tromps through the mixed softwoods, hardwoods and aspen of the area. Still, it was the third day of the deer rifle season, and McCombs was leery of running into some out-of-state hunter on this public land who might use the dog's antics as an excuse to take a shot at it.

As he had known that it would, the dog gave up the chase shortly thereafter and trotted back to McCombs, well pleased with itself. McCombs watched it return to him with a mixture of equal affection and aggravation. Sam, the springer spaniel, would hunt anything: grouse, mice, deer, bear, it made little difference to the dog. More than once, McCombs had to intercede between the dog and a curious fisher. It still hadn't learned, at five years old, that porcupines were to be avoided.

McCombs had been warned, when he bought the pup at five weeks old, that the Eagle River breed of springer spaniel was hyperactive until the day that they died, but he had been unaware that they were also completely demented. Weighing a lean forty pounds, the spaniel was a tightly wound bundle of nervous energy that, if nothing else more amusing was available, would chase sunbeams all day long until it dropped from sheer exhaustion.

Still, McCombs thought, it was a thing of beauty to watch the dog at work in a thicket, with its impressive olfactory equipment, searching out any faint scent. While the dog worked, McCombs would wait for the occasional ruffed grouse to come rocketing out of the thicket, with his tiny double-barreled twenty-gauge shotgun at the ready. Not that he could hit much anymore, he reflected ruefully; at sixty years old, his hand-eye coordination was a thing of the past. The spaniel never seemed to care too much about his poor aim, though; for the dog, the hunt was the important thing.

But, today McCombs had more important things to take care of, because it was high time to look up Carl Lemke. The dog would definitely be in the way.

The massive blast over Superior two days previously, a detonation that had rattled the windows in his Ontonagon home, had rattled McCombs much more severely than his house, since it had come so soon on the heels of 9/11. Even more so than the terrorist attack on 'The Twin Towers', the explosion had brought home not only to him but also to every resident of the Upper Peninsula that they were not insulated from world events; even up here, so far from the mainstream of American life.

The local media had dutifully published the official version of the cause of the explosion, an improperly vented ship's hold, but McCombs did not believe it for a second. A Viet Nam veteran, McCombs had heard the concussion of high explosive military ordinance, close at hand, before. The potential horrors that McCombs had retired to Ontonagon to avoid now seemed to be staring him directly in the face.

McCombs needed a stiff drink. Lemke could not only provide that, but perhaps he could also provide some intelligent perspective on the events of the past months.

As the dog trotted back to him, McCombs called out to the animal, "Ride in truck, Sam," as he opened the passenger side door of the beat-up pickup truck. Without hesitation the dog sprang up on the seat, ready for the next adventure, as McCombs closed the door behind him. Glancing over his shoulder as he walked away, McCombs saw the spaniel looking at him with an expression of complete betrayal, through the opaque passenger-side window that was covered with dog slobber and nose prints, as he returned to the creek bottom. He'll get over it, McCombs thought to himself, a little guiltily.

McCombs had stumbled across the Lemke camp a few years before on an exploratory bird hunting trip with Sam, then still a young pup. The camp was well off the forest road. The easiest way to get to it, without blocking the faint two-track going in, was to walk the creek bottom for nearly a mile, before cutting north through an aspen grove of several different year classes.

McCombs never hunted deer anymore, and he was not hunting this day, for grouse hunting was closed for the duration of rifle season. He carried no weapon, and therefore he had not bothered to wear hunter orange, opting instead for his usual Carhart bibs and earth-colored fleece-lined shirt on this warm fall day. McCombs hated wearing orange, even though required by law, anytime; in a quiet rebellion, as he thought of it, against mindless, unenforceable regulations.

McCombs had never quite bought into the notion that most game species were color-blind. He privately thought that walking around in the woods, blazing in the sunlight like a neon sign, just made him a better target, in this age when most hunters got out into the woods and handled a weapon for only a few days a year. McCombs would rather take his chances and depend on his woods sense to keep him out of trouble.

As he walked quietly in the creek bottom, McCombs remembered that first chance meeting with Lemke. He had stood on the aspen ridge as the spaniel rummaged through the underbrush. He had looked down into the camp, a large camp that looked capable of sheltering a dozen or more hunters. That day, however, there had only been one vehicle in the large yard, for it was still two weeks before rifle season: an old pickup truck with a camper on back, hooked with its hitch to a large enclosed snowmobile trailer and parked next to what he had taken at first to be a sauna, a low building with wood smoke curling from its stovepipe chimney.

As McCombs recalled, just then the door to the 'sauna' had swung open, and a fantastic apparition had walked out into the yard. It was a tall, sandy-haired, spare-framed man with a bobcat fur hat on his head. The hat's paws hung down over the man's ears like flaps, and its head, eyes, and grinning teeth faced forward.

The man had been dressed in a flannel shirt and some nondescript pants, with red suspenders. He had worn the tallest leather leggings that McCombs had ever seen, leggings that extended almost to the man's crotch, with gray woolen balls that hung from the periphery of each legging at the top. At the time, McCombs hadn't known whether to laugh out loud or to keep silent in stunned amazement. And then, the dog had noticed the man and had barked. The man had looked up to the aspen ridge, and he had seen them, man and dog, standing there. He had then gestured them to join him in the yard.

The two men had hit it off immediately. Carl Lemke was about the same age as he was, McCombs figured; but Lemke was one of those rare, wiry, and apparently ageless men who could be anywhere between fifty and eighty, lean almost to the point of being dried up.

He was a process engineer at one of the big Detroit automakers, he had told McCombs. The camp had been in his family for several generations. Normally, he had said, he wore a white shirt and tie, with a pocket protector stuffed full of pens and calculating and measuring devices, a straight arrow who went to church every Sunday and who never uttered a curse word. When he came to camp each fall, however, he "liked to let his hair down a little."

Lemke had told him that he always had a camp full of relatives and friends for the rifle season. He liked to precede the rest of the crew by a couple of weeks, to cut firewood and enjoy the place by himself. Noticing

McCombs glancing at the gray woolen balls at the tops of his leggings, Lemke had jokingly referred to them as his "dingleberries". His wife had made them for him years ago, he explained, saying that if he wanted to act as crazy as a loon, he might as well look the part.

As the conversation ebbed and flowed over the next hour, the men had warmed to each other. Lemke had a wide-ranging intellect, and he had interesting opinions on a variety of subjects. Even Sam the spaniel, an animal that normally tolerated no human being other than McCombs, had liked Lemke immediately, due in no small part to the steak bone that the man had produced from somewhere.

As the dog lolled in the grass of the yard, blissfully gnawing on the morsel, Lemke had produced a half-gallon fruit jar of clear fluid and had asked McCombs if he'd care to indulge in "a wee snort"; and, as it was already well past noon, McCombs had allowed that he wouldn't mind. McCombs still remembered that moment of bliss clearly, as the jar had contained the finest corn sipping whiskey that he had ever sampled. For Carl Lemke, process engineer and straight arrow, was, at his camp at least, an amateur moonshiner.

Lemke had shown him around. The snowmobile trailer was full of one hundred-pound bags of shell corn and fifty-pound bags of sugar, along with assorted bags of distiller's yeast. Some of the corn would be used to bait the camp's deer blinds, Lemke had told him, but the rest was reserved for his liquid hobby. Lemke didn't hunt at all anymore, he had told McCombs. He left that for the younger men, while he concentrated solely on producing a year's worth of sipping whiskey during his time at camp.

What McCombs had taken to be a sauna was actually the building that housed Lemke's still. Inside, a stainless steel, thirty-gallon milk can that served as the boiler sat atop an old cast-iron, wood-fired cook stove. From the lid of the milk can protruded a cracking tower of two-inch copper pipe that was filled with stainless steel packing. At the top of the pipe, a small hole conducted the rising alcohol vapors to a condenser of copper tubes, surrounded by cold water from the camp's well. Once condensed, the alcohol, now a liquid, was collected and refined in several filtering operations. Containers of sprouting corn in various stages of fermentation were everywhere. A dryer and a large grinder for making meal of the sprouted corn, to convert it into mash, stood along one wall.

Lemke wasn't particularly concerned with getting caught, he had confided to McCombs. The camp received few visitors, except the regulars, even by accident due to its remote location. Besides, he had said, it wasn't as if he were doing anything that the authorities actually cared about, like raising a surreptitious patch of marijuana or running a 'cat' lab, as methamphetamine was known locally.

Additionally, Lemke had confided, it felt good to actually take a minor risk in his otherwise orderly and disciplined life, and he could easily afford the fine in any event. In fact, several judges and law enforcement officials in the Detroit area regularly sampled his product, he had asserted. McCombs didn't doubt him for an instant.

Lemke didn't permit hunting anywhere on the forty acres of property immediately surrounding the camp, he had told McCombs, saying that the deer were so enamored of the used-up corn mash that he dumped in a small ravine behind the still that it just wasn't sporting. Besides, he had said emphatically, the camp was surrounded by close to a million acres of national forest; the lazy buggers that shared his camp during the rifle season could find their own deer out there on public land, like everybody else.

Each subsequent fall since then, McCombs had made this trip down the creek bottom, to see how Lemke had weathered the previous winter, to be engaged in lively conversation, and to sample his wonderful 'mountain dew', usually to the point of being over-served. For McCombs, it had become a seasonal highlight, like the geese winging south and the sandhill cranes gathering west of the camp in the close-cropped fields back of Mass.

In short order, McCombs had reached his destination and then he cut north to the ridge overlooking the camp. The aspen had been clear-cut in a Forest Service timber sale the previous summer. The ridge was a moonscape: a gutted, barren scene of desolation, with deeply scarred trenches everywhere in the red soil that looked like raw wounds, and with loose stumps and discarded aspen scraps stacked in tangled masses everywhere. Although McCombs well understood the logic for clear-cutting aspen, a strategy essential for its subsequent regeneration, and while he knew that in ten years or a little more the area would be a vibrant haven for wildlife, the immediate aftermath of this logging practice was never very pretty to see.

As he reached the ridge, McCombs looked down into the yard of the big camp. Looked like Lemke had the usual crew here this year, he thought to himself, as he surveyed eight trucks and SUVs with Michigan and Wisconsin license plates; but, as he started down the ridge, he stopped short. Something was out of place here, a voice in the back of his mind told him; the hairs briefly stood up on the back of his neck.

Below, two men walked back and forth between the camp and the vehicles, performing some chore. McCombs didn't recognize either of them; these men were stockier than his previous acquaintances. They carried on whatever they were doing in silence, instead of the usual light banter one normally heard in a deer camp. McCombs could see Lemke's old pickup parked next to the building that housed the still, but no wood smoke curled out of the stovepipe chimney.

Lemke had probably had to go to town for some reason with one of the others, he reasoned. Well, he thought, with no particular concern, no point in making his presence known to these strangers, as he made his way quietly back up the ridge. A vague suspicion still gnawed at him, but he dismissed it as just being jumpy over recent events. Besides, Lemke would be at the camp for at least a week after the end of rifle season, as was his usual practice, so there would be plenty of time to get reacquainted.

After making his way back upstream along the creek bottom to his truck, McCombs found Sam the springer spaniel sulking on the seat in silence, as if he would never have another kind thought about the man who had so briefly abandoned him. Grateful for the momentary quiet, McCombs started the old pickup and made his way north and west along the forest roads, taking the scenic route back to his home in Ontonagon, and knowing that the dog would revert to his usual demented self when they got within a half-mile of the house. The late fall afternoon sun was warm, and dust devils danced in the wake of the truck.

*   *   *   *

The telephone on Sidney Hornberg's desk in his Marquette FBI office rang, as a dozen other people bent to their laptop computers and instruments. After three rings, when all were ready, he picked up the phone and answered "Hornberg," flatly into the receiver.

"Gregor here, Mr. Hornberg. Good afternoon," the disembodied voice replied.

"Gregor, you seem to know a lot about our GPS satellite tracking ability," said Hornberg, a slight question framed by his inflection, referring to the mystery man's previous call from the Marquette Wal-Mart parking lot.

"Indeed, Mr. Hornberg, I do. It is, I think you would say, a result of a life's work," the voice responded, with a hint of humor.

"Gregor," Hornberg asked, in a serious tone, as the other officials listened closely, "I must ask you. Why did you explode that device on Lake Superior?"

"It was necessary, Mr. Hornberg, to demonstrate our bonafides, to show you not only what we possess but that we know how to detonate them," the voice replied calmly. "And," the voice went on, calmly and rationally, "you should note that we tried to do it in a manner that would minimize the necessary damage."

"Gregor," Hornberg replied accusingly, "you killed twenty-two innocent people!"

"Ah yes, the two Native American people on shore," the voice mechanically replied. "That was unintentional, we could not have known about them."

This guy is good, Hornberg thought, quietly. The search teams had only this morning discovered the few shards of human flesh and clothing in the massive destruction below Fourteen-Mile Point that was all that was left of the old man on the beach, and the mess inside the wrecked vehicle at the Firesteel bridge had deliberately not been made known to the public.

"As for the rest," the voice continued—Hornberg could almost see the man's unconscious shrug in his mind's eye—"they were sailors, and soldiers and sailors die. It is the nature of their occupation and their principal reason for existing. If we had not killed them, they would have died some other way, at some other time."

"That is cold, Gregor," said Hornberg, in sudden revulsion.

"Yes, well, life is cold, Mr. Hornberg," the voice replied logically. "For the moment, you need only to know that we possess other identical devices. Goodbye for now, you must be close to locking in on my position. We shall talk again soon." And then the connection went dead.

This time, the discarded cell phone was found on a picnic table at a rest area on State Highway M-95, some five miles south of the small village of Republic. No fingerprints were found on the phone, and the dry dust of the rest area revealed nothing of the vehicle that the man might have used.

CHAPTER 5

▼

As he did almost every weeknight now and had for some time, Sidney Hornberg sat in his lazy-boy chair in his north Marquette home, hard by Northern Michigan University, staring holes in the ceiling. As usual, he awaited the sleep that he knew would not come easily this night, even with the sleeping pill and the several stiff pulls he had taken off the bottle of whiskey in the cupboard. He was drinking more now, more each night.

The events of the previous day played over and over through Hornberg's thoughts. This 'Gregor', terrorist or whatever he was, would likely be the straw that would finally break his fragile state of mind, the latest in a long series of demons that had sapped his strength and had driven his blood pressure to dangerous levels. By the sound of his voice and by his actions to date, the man was completely ruthless and remorseless.

Hornberg was despondent. I am no kind of man anymore, he thought, morosely. I am unable to concentrate at work, unable to sleep, unable to physically satisfy my wife. In a few months my career will be over, and then what will be left, he asked his inner muse? What will take the place of what I have done all of my adult life, he beseeched the angel of his Jewish childhood, *Sar ha-Panim*? But the Prince of the Presence, having been rejected so often by Hornberg over his lifetime, refused to be summoned, and the questions remained unanswered.

The phone ringing on the table next to his lazy-boy interrupted Hornberg's morbid thoughts. He picked it up quickly to avoid waking his wife upstairs, after having punched the recorder that the Bureau had insisted that he attach to his home phone to the 'on' position. 'Hornberg residence," he said wearily into the receiver in the darkness.

"Good morning, Mr. Hornberg, Gregor here," the now familiar voice said, lightly. "Can't sleep?"

"How did you get this number, Gregor?" Hornberg asked, in unfeigned surprise. His home phone number was unlisted.

"Child's play, Mr. Hornberg, as you are well aware," the voice replied. "You must not take me for a fool, for I too know of these things. May I please call you 'Sidney'?" he continued, casually. "'Mr. Hornberg' seems so overly formal, under the circumstances."

"What do you want from me, Gregor?" Hornberg asked, his irritation now genuine.

"What I want, Sidney, is to have a reasonable conversation with a reasonable man, with enough time to do so without having to worry about armed men dropping out of the sky onto my position," Gregor continued patently. "Not only that, but these cell phones that I keep throwing away are getting to be a bit expensive", he added lightly.

"I presume, Sidney, that you have some sort of phone recorder activated right now as we speak," continued Gregor, in a business-like tone, "and that is fine, for I want you to get what I tell you exactly correct. However," he added offhandedly, "I am wagering that you do not have your satellite tracking equipment attached to your home phone. That might make for some disagreeable domestic circumstances, yes?" the disembodied voice chuckled softly.

"Why me?" asked Hornberg, almost plaintively. "Why not speak to somebody at a higher level? I'm just a low level FBI agent in a small northern Michigan city," he went on, exasperated. "I can't do anything for you, and I'm not authorized to speak for my government."

"On the contrary, Sidney, you are exactly the person to whom I wish to speak," Gregor replied, in a conciliatory tone. "We are very much alike, you and I. We are both the products of our respective systems, and we are both at the end of our respective lines, so to speak," he continued, as if sharing a confidence.

"Sidney, I think that we both understand disappointment, and despair, and great fear, and lost hope," Gregor continued, piously. "I also believe that you will communicate my message to your government exactly, without embellishment as some of your young lions might be tempted to do," he added accusingly. "It is important to your country that it understands my meaning precisely."

"Even if I were the person that you have described, you must already know that my country never does business with terrorists," Hornberg replied, acidly.

"Sidney," the man called Gregor replied, a flinty edge suddenly in his voice, "apparently I must make an important distinction for you. Understand this now, and remember it always! We are not terrorists!" he barked.

"A terrorist is motivated by ideology, and for him the terror is an end in itself," Gregor continued, like a teacher rebuking a slow student. "The terrorist wants to make you believe that, if you accept his ideology, whatever that might be, the terror will end."

"No, Sidney, we are far more dangerous than terrorists, for we are motivated by much more practical matters," Gregor went on. "We are murderers, thieves and extortionists, all of this is true—but we are not terrorists! And Sidney," the voice concluded, now more calmly, "your government routinely does business with murderers, thieves and extortionists every day, all over the world, as does mine."

Hornberg collapsed inwardly at the man's harsh judgment. This 'Gregor' was speaking the truth, and he knew it. "What is it that you want to tell me, Gregor?" he now replied, weakly.

"The device that was exploded three days ago," Gregor replied, much more calmly now, "was a device that went missing from the Russian National Nuclear Weapons Storage Facility at Golovchino, a few miles from Ukraine, in the winter of 1998. It was a one hundred fifty-five millimeter artillery shell of the Koshevoy series, one of the oldest models in the former Soviet arsenal," the man continued, matter-of-factly. "We also maintain possession of similar devices."

Gregor then rattled off a long serial number. I hope the recorder got that, Hornberg thought frantically. His mind was racing with the implications of the man's words.

"You will need to get your Intelligence Community involved to verify the truth of what I have told you, Sidney," Gregor continued, casually. "The Russians will be loath to admit to the former lax security at their nuclear weapons storage sites."

"What do you expect to gain from this, Gregor"? Hornberg asked, genuinely perplexed. "Do you think that you can hold the Upper Peninsula of Michigan hostage, with some old Russian nuke artillery shells, and get America to spring for big bucks?"

"All in good time, Sidney, all in good time," the man replied calmly. "But in partial answer to your question, no, our goal is not monetary. If that had been the case," he explained logically, "we could have easily turned these weapons over to any number of factions that sincerely desire your country's destruction, for any amount of money that we might have demanded, without having to incur the risks that we have so far. And no, your beautiful Upper Peninsula holds no particular interest for us; it was simply the easiest point of entry into your country," Gregor concluded.

"Then, what do you want?" demanded Hornberg.

"Sidney, I think it is time that we meet," Gregor replied firmly. "The rest of our discussion will be technically complicated, and it is best carried on face to face. There are matters to discuss that will require considerable explanation."

"I shall give you a few days to digest the information you now have, and then I will propose a meeting between us," Gregor went on. "But only with you, Sidney," the man warned. "No one else."

"You should also know that the remaining devices in our possession are no longer located in the Upper Peninsula. They have been moved to different large Midwest cities," Gregor went on, in a chilling voice.

"And Sidney," the man continued ominously, "the people who guard the devices in these locations are people whom I trust implicitly. They are under my orders to automatically detonate the devices if they do not hear from me every three hours."

And then the line went dead.

*   *   *   *

Sidney Hornberg and Paul Adams, the Michigan State Police detective from Houghton, sat in Hornberg's Marquette FBI office, awaiting their visitors. The Bureau's Director had specifically requested Adams' presence, in an unusual request to the Michigan Governor, to assist in the current investigation.

Hornberg had just played the recording of his discussion with Gregor on his home phone during the previous morning for Adams. Both men now sat quietly, in stunned silence. There didn't seem to be much to add, they both seemed to think. Both men's minds wandered about, searching vainly for answers that didn't exist.

An announcement by Hornberg's secretary suddenly interrupted their reverie. Hornberg went to the door to admit the two men, one in the uniform of a full Army colonel and the other in a casual business suit.

The man in the suit did the introductions for the strangers. He was Bruce Wilton, from the Directorate of Operations for the Central Intelligence Agency. His companion was Colonel Frank Wenzel, of the Office of the Deputy Chief of Staff, Intelligence-G2 of the United States Army. Hornberg introduced Adams, and then the four men retired to beat-up chairs in Hornberg's small office to begin their discussion.

"Well, Mr. Hornberg," began Wilton, in an opening gambit, "We've spent some time listening to your conversations with this 'Gregor' fellow. It certainly would appear that you have opened a huge, stinking can of worms," he said, with a slight smirk.

"And just how did I do that, Mr. Wilton?" asked Hornberg, defensively. "Just by being assigned to this Marquette office?"

"Just so, Mr. Hornberg, just so," replied the CIA man, emphatically. "This operation was obviously carefully planned for several years."

"These people knew precisely the easiest route and means to smuggle fissile material into this country," Wilton went on. "And, for whatever reason, the leader of this operation has decided that you, Sidney Hornberg, are going to be the conduit for his 'message', or whatever it is that he wants."

"Well, what do we really know about his claims?" asked Hornberg, with some exasperation. "Does he have what he says he does?"

"So it would appear," Wilton continued, matter-of-factly. "I must tell you both now," he continued in a low, conspiratorial voice, "that what I am about to tell you is classified to the highest level. You are now both considered cleared for 'Top Secret'. You may find that this is not necessarily the privilege that you may mistake it for," he added, with a slight, frigid smile

"At any rate," Wilton continued amiably, as Hornberg and Adams exchanged quick glances, "we do know that the artillery shell that this 'Gregor' gave you the serial number of did in fact go missing from the Golovchino National Nuclear Weapons Storage facility in Russia, as the man said, in the winter of 1998. It is not necessary for you to know how we know this," he went on, briskly, "but it has been verified to our satisfaction."

Unfortunately," Wilton continued somberly, "it was not the only nuclear device to go missing from the former Soviet storage facilities at about this time. The Russians have many nuclear weapons storage facilities, all over Russia," Wilton explained, "that contain all or most of the tactical nuclear warheads removed from the former Soviet block countries at the end of the Cold War; several thousand devices: torpedo warheads, depth charges, artillery shells, land mines, surface-to-air and air-to-air missile warheads."

"Where all these warheads are, we do not know," Wilton said, quietly. "We suspect that not even the Russians know, nor even how many they had in the first place. The warhead that we are now discussing apparently got lost in the confusion."

As the men absorbed this chilling information, Hornberg asked, "What do we know about the specific weapon that Gregor claims to have set off?"

Wilton deferred to Colonel Wenzel. "Well," said Wenzel, quickly referring to notes in the briefcase on his lap, "we know that the Koshevoy series of one hundred fifty-five millimeter nuclear artillery shells was one of the first 'production model' nuclear weapons made for the Red Army. Several thousand of them were produced."

"The Koshevoy was a simple warhead by today's standards," Wenzel went on. "It had none of the electronic locking mechanisms present in today's weapons, the ones that will automatically disable themselves if tampered with, or the artillery shell firing mechanism that must be switched on by the act of being fired from a cannon in order to be detonated."

"These old warheads were basically impact weapons," Wenzel stated, flatly. "They could probably be detonated by firing a forty-five caliber pistol into the firing mechanism."

But these things must be heavy, right?" asked Adams, quizzically. "Hard to transport, hard to move around?"

"Unfortunately no," replied Colonel Wenzel, with a deadpan expression. "Even by today's standards, these weapons were not much bigger than a standard one hundred fifty-five millimeter artillery shell. They were about thirty-four inches long and weighed about one hundred pounds or a little better. Any man in good shape," he added dryly, looking at Adams' burley figure, "could easily pick one up and carry it for long distances."

"But the radiation shielding?" asked Hornberg, puzzled. "Doesn't that increase the overall weight of the weapon?"

"Very few nuclear artillery shells employ shielding of any kind, Mr. Hornberg," replied Colonel Wenzel, with a slight smile, like an indulgent teacher explaining a simple problem to a slow student. "Most of the mass of the shell is steel. This is more than ample shielding for the critical mass of the fissile plutonium within it that may be not much larger than a grapefruit and weigh ten pounds, or maybe a little less."

"But wouldn't the radioactive plutonium decay away after all these years in storage?" continued Hornberg. He knew that he was pressing the limit of his knowledge.

"Wishful thinking, sir," answered Wenzel. "The half-life of plutonium-239 is twenty-four thousand years."

"What kind of damage could something like this cause in a city environment?" pressed Adams, fatalistically, thinking of the almost nine million people living in Michigan alone.

"Well, sir," said the colonel, his face drawn, "the best comparison that I can give you is that, if one of these shells were to be set off in the University of Michigan football stadium on game day, everyone not at the concession stands, which are behind concrete pilings, would be dead immediately."

"Also," Wenzel added, as Adams was still grappling with the stadium comparison, "anyone in a restroom, or getting a hot dog, or walking past the stadium on the street, would be dead within a few days of the explosion. Add to that number the firemen, police, and rescue workers who would inevitably respond," he continued in a dread voice, "and you might be talking about a hundred thousand casualties, or maybe more."

The room was suddenly enveloped with a dark silence as Hornberg and Adams struggled with the images. Then the CIA man, Wilton, spoke. "Mr. Hornberg, Mr. Adams," he said, as he addressed them; "you are advised that this is now a National Security Agency operation. As the ranking member of the Intelligence Community on scene, I am in charge. You will both take your orders from me, directly."

"Adams, you know the ground, and this is why we asked for you, specifically," Wilton said to the Michigan State Police detective. "And as for you, Hornberg," he added almost whimsically, "I would not want to be in your shoes."

After several pensive moments in the abruptly silent room, Wilton continued, abstractly, "So, Hornberg, have you given any thought to this meeting that 'Gregor" proposes?"

"Not really," Hornberg stated absently. "I probably won't hear from him for a few days, but based on his actions so far he doesn't seem like the kind of guy that we want to screw with. He almost seems…"

"Professional?" Wilton quickly replied, finishing Hornberg's thought. "Somebody more than just some rogue terrorist who happened to luck into some Russian nuclear warheads?"

"Exactly," responded Hornberg, raising his eyebrows slightly in surprise. "He seems to be way too dialed into the way intelligence is conducted, and he seems to know things about me personally that nobody else knows," he concluded.

"We've had the same thought, after listening to your taped conversations with him," Wilton responded, with a slight smile and a nod towards Colonel Wenzel. "We've even begun to think that he might be a military or an intelligence man. Tell me, Hornberg, what do you know of the Russian GRU?" asked Wilton, seemingly out of curiosity.

"Nothing much," Hornberg replied, almost apologetically. "We don't do a lot of business with them here in Marquette," he added, sarcastically.

"So you may think, Hornberg, but they may know much more about you than you would find comfortable," Wilton replied, acidly. "Colonel Wenzel, could you give them a thumbnail sketch?"

"The Main Intelligence Directorate of the Russian military, the *Glavnoye Razvedyvatelnoye Upravleniye*, or GRU, is Russia's primary and most capable intelligence agency, with thousands of agents all over the world," Wenzel began, with practiced ease. "The GRU has complete command over all of the intelligence-gathering resources of the Russian armed forces, and they are subordinate only to the Russian Defense Minister and the Chief of General Staff of the armed forces."

"The GRU does not report to the political leadership of Russia," Wenzel continued, no longer referring to his notes. "Even Russia's top civilian government members can only get access to GRU information through the Defense Minister of the Chief of General Staff."

"The GRU," Wenzel continued, with the professional admiration of his Russian counterparts readily evident, "possesses the largest and most elite group of special operations forces in the Russian army, with at least twenty-four assault units numbering up to twenty-five thousand troops. Only the most elite and senior soldiers, highly educated and fluent in several languages, with years of special operations experience, serve in the GRU. During the Soviet era," Wenzel concluded, with his face slightly flushed, "the number of agents operated throughout the world by the Russian GRU was six times the number of agents operated by the Soviet KGB."

Hornberg and Adams were both impressed. "So you think that this 'Gregor' guy is a GRU man?" asked Adams, curiously.

"It's possible," replied Wilton, with a shrug. "He seems to fit the profile. His movements so far seem to be like those of our own special operations people His English is perfect—no slang, no regional inflections or dialect of any kind that our experts can tell from the tapes."

"Our Colonel Wenzel here speaks Russian in much the same way. His Russian is actually much better than his English," Wilton added, sarcastically, with a nod and a smile towards the Army man, who replied with a small tight grin. Brought up in Negaunee before his appointment to West Point, Frank Wenzel was notorious among his intelligence colleagues for the fact that his speech occasionally lapsed into 'Yoopereese' when he had been over-served in the Officer's Mess.

"Even in post-Cold War Russia, I wonder," Wilton continued, as if talking to himself. "How easy could it have been to walk into a nuclear weapons storage facility, collect a few nuclear artillery shells, walk back out again, transport the warheads across international boundaries, and conceal them for three years?" he asked, almost rhetorically.

"No, this guy had a network; he knew the way into Golovchino, and he had a way out," Wilton concluded. "And he's still working his plan now, for purposes we do not yet know."

An awful thought suddenly occurred to Hornberg. "But if he's a Russian military man, wouldn't that make this explosion on Lake Superior…"

"An act of war against the United States by Russia?" Wilton answered Hornberg's question again, unbidden. "Exactly so, Mr. Hornberg, exactly so!"

CHAPTER 6

▼

It was a few hours after sunset, and Sidney Hornberg was boring a hole through the Upper Peninsula black night, westward on U.S. Highway 41 just past the small tourist town of Michigamme. He was in a small government sedan, on his way to a meeting with a man whom he had never met, under conditions that he had absolutely no control over.

Very few lights of any kind illuminated the roadway, except at the occasional intersection with a county road. But, it was a mostly clear night, and the vast blanket of stars and a half-moon cast enough light to throw the backdrop of hills and valleys that were covered with hardwoods and interspersed here and there with various species of conifers, into a black-and-white stark panorama for as far as the eye could see, for the first snow of the season had finally fallen. It would have been a beautiful drive tonight under other circumstances, he thought; Emma would have loved it.

He thought of his wife now with fondness. She had come up behind him, unnoticed, as he had sat at the desktop computer in their Marquette home before he had left on this night. She had observed quietly as he went quickly through their personal files that contained his Federal pension arrangements, his will, their investments, and their mortgage and insurance information, and then had jotted short notes down longhand on a list that also contained a number of names and telephone numbers. At last, she had said quietly, "It's the Ontonagon thing, isn't it?"

Startled, he had glanced at her quickly over his shoulder and then had seemed to collapse into himself. "Yes, Emma, it is," he had replied quietly. "I'm going out tonight, and I don't know where I'm going or when I'll be back. I just wanted to make sure that you knew where this stuff was in case something unexpected happens. "Better safe than sorry," he concluded weakly.

Emma had placed her hands gently on his shoulders. "Sidney, I'm your wife," she had said softly. "Who do you think you're fooling? You've never done this before."

"Well, dear, I've never felt so not in control before," he had replied, as if he was completely unnerved.

Emma had regarded him fondly. She was well aware of her husband's sleepless nights, and the ever increasing drinking, and his gradual physical withdrawal from her. Before this night she had attributed these things to some sort of middle-aged angst on her husband's part; a ritual of passage, perhaps, a final goodbye to youth, and career, and hopes and aspirations. But now she had seen something that she had never observed in him before: fear, stark fear. Of what, she had no idea.

Her steadfast FBI husband, the man who she had heard so many stories about from his colleagues and their wives, about the bullet marks and various scars on his body that she had kissed so ardently during their courtship not so many years ago; this man was deeply afraid of something unknown, at least to her. At that moment, she had suddenly understood her husband as never before. Lovingly, she had then taken his head in her hands and had buried it comfortably between her breasts, stroking his hair and saying not a word.

Hornberg now put the thoughts of his wife out of his mind and reflected on the events of the past few days as he drove down the darkened roadway. The discussion of possible Russian involvement in this bizarre event was still difficult for Hornberg to come to grips with, since the Cold War was long since past. Talk of burgeoning democracy in the former Soviet republics was now on the lips of all of the television 'talking heads'.

Without further information from this 'Gregor', it was impossible to even guess who might be involved or even what they were looking for. The threats that the mystery man had made might well be bluffs for some reason, but no one in an official capacity could afford to make that assumption with so many civilian lives at risk.

The officials involved at all levels strongly suspected that at least one of the conspirators, perhaps 'Gregor' himself, was still in the immediate area. Unfortunately, so were a hundred thousand out-of-state and out-of-area hunters, in addition to the locals, all involved in the yearly ritual of the deer rifle season and all of whom, as Paul Adams had put it succinctly, were "armed to the teeth". Strange faces were the norm at this time of the year in the Upper Peninsula.

Finding a one hundred pound nuclear artillery shell in a package no bigger than a backpack, one that emitted no readily discernable radiation, in one of the many large Midwest cities within easy driving distance was like searching for the proverbial needle in a haystack. Disaster agencies in the whole area had been quietly warned to prepare for the worst.

But finally, the call had come in to Hornberg's Marquette FBI office late that afternoon, as they had known all along that it must. Hornberg replayed it through his mind now as he drove, just as it had been received, as dozens of technicians had officials had listened in on their tracing and tracking equipment.

"Good afternoon, Sidney, Gregor here," the familiar voice had intoned, lightly, as if he were discussing a date for lunch. "I take it that you have had sufficient time to corroborate the information about what we possess?"

Hornberg had stuck to the script as the CIA man, Wilton, had given it to him. The Russian military, he had been told, had been furious, in conversations with their American counterparts, at the subtle suggestion that they might somehow unwittingly be complicit in this matter.

"In general, Gregor, your information seems to be accurate," Hornberg had replied, with no apparent inflection. "We shall choose to take you at your word for the moment. However," he had added, carefully, drawing it out to keep the man on the line as long as possible, "you still haven't given us any indication about what it is that you want."

"Exactly why we must now meet, Sidney," Gregor had replied expansively. "Tonight. You are to leave your home in Marquette at precisely

1900 hours and drive west on U.S. Highway 41, alone. We will be monitoring your progress. Your cell phone number, please?"

Hornberg had given him the number. Gregor had then continued, "Once we have verified that you are indeed alone and are not being followed, we will contact you with updated instructions. Please do not bring any weapons, not even your famous pocket knife!" Gregor added, in an apparent attempt at levity.

"We have no wish to harm you, Sidney, but you will be carefully searched," Gregor went on. "And, I suppose that it would be naïve of me to expect that your people will not attempt to place some sort of locating device on either you or your vehicle. I assure you that it will do them no good."

"Additionally," Gregor had added, grimly, while pausing for emphasis; "I must reiterate what you already know. If my associates in your large Midwestern cities where the other devices are presently located do not hear from me every three hours, they will be automatically detonated with no further direction from me."

And then the line had gone dead. This time, the discarded cell phone would eventually be tracked to a roadside ditch on a county road north of Sidnaw, but not until much later.

Hornberg now let his mind freewheel, alone on the dark road as he drove west. The various agencies had discussed endless possibilities about using tracking devices, or very loose tails. They had all been dismissed as too risky, for they simply could not afford to panic this quarry.

The recorder taped to his chest beneath his left armpit had twelve hours of capacity, he had been told by the CIA expert. There was nothing to be done now but wait for instructions as he had been directed.

The moonlight was almost bright enough to read by as the beam of his headlights briefly captured a road sign proclaiming a public access at Parent Lake. Just then, the cell phone jangled in his pocket.

Pulling out the phone's antenna with his teeth, he answered, quickly, "Hornberg."

Just as quickly, a voice replied, "Left on M-28, three miles," and then hung up.

Hornberg stared briefly at the phone. Less than three seconds, he thought; not much chance of the NASA folks getting a satellite fix on that conversation.

After making the turn onto M-28 at a wide intersection, where an overhead crane stood and log cabin-making debris was scattered across the landscape, Hornberg continued westward through the tiny communities of Covington, and then Watton, before his cell phone chirped again. This time, before he had a chance to say anything, the voice told him, "Right on Forest Road 2200, four miles," before hanging up.

A few miles later, just as lights in the near distance greeted his approach to the old lumbering community of Sidnaw, he saw signs to his right proclaiming the 'Sturgeon River Gorge Wilderness' and Forest Road 2200. Turning to the north, he drove down the good sand road past several camps, before the forest closed over him and the night became completely dark.

After a mile or so, Hornberg was jolted by the glare of a dash-mounted police light in his rear-view mirror. Yeah, sure, it's a county cop, he thought to himself, sarcastically, as he pulled to the side of the dark dirt road. The vehicle with the light pulled in behind him as a second, darkened vehicle pulled in front of him and blocked his exit.

Hornberg sat quietly, awaiting direction, until an automatic machine pistol rapped at his driver-side window: '*tap, tap, tap*' in quick succession. As he lowered the window, the passenger-side door opened. A black-clothed figure in a ski mask slid on to the seat beside him, while the man at his left placed the machine pistol, almost gently, behind his left ear.

The man on the seat beside him searched him quickly but expertly and pulled up his shirt to examine the recorder beneath his armpit closely. The two men briefly conversed in a language he did not understand. Then, the familiar voice of Gregor said, from the darkness behind the machine pistol, in perfect English: "Sidney, please remove your belt and your shoes and empty your pockets on the front seat. All very slowly and carefully, please."

After Hornberg had done as he had been directed, Gregor opened the driver's side door and took him by the arm. He carefully extracted Hornberg from the car, while keeping the machine pistol at his head. Hornberg gasped as the cold night air assaulted his lungs, while his feet, in their stockings, slogged through several inches of new snow.

After being joined by the other man, the two then bent Hornberg over the hood of the car and bound his hands behind him with duct tape. They then wrapped duct tape about his head, over his eyes, to serve as a blindfold. The tall man then pressed a liquid-saturated handkerchief to Hornberg's face for fifteen seconds, until his body went limp.

Carrying Hornberg's inert body, the two men carefully lifted him up onto the high bench seat of a large pickup truck, the light on its dash still flashing, behind his government vehicle. One of them then slid a heavy pair of woolen socks over Hornberg's feet and draped a blanket about his shoulders.

The driver threw the big truck in gear and pulled around Hornberg's car in the original northerly direction in a spray of sand and gravel, at a high rate of speed. Several miles had passed before a violent turn to the left jammed Hornberg into the passenger-side door. The impact jolted Hornberg awake.

As he slowly came to his senses, Hornberg found himself tilted to his right on the high bench seat, with a headache and with a foul taste in his mouth. After Hornberg had stiffly and awkwardly regained his seating, not having the use of his hands, the tall man said to him from the driver side, calmly, "Sorry about the sedative, Sidney, but it was only intended to be momentary, until we knew that you were under control. I'm sure you understand." His words registered fuzzily on Hornberg's mind.

"You've done well so far, Sidney," the hooded figure continued, in faint praise. "We have examined your recorder, and we are satisfied that it does not contain any tracking mechanisms. You are welcome to keep it, for you need to get the details of our meeting correct."

"What details, Gregor?" Hornberg replied thickly, as if he had a mouth full of cotton. 'Detail' was one of several things he didn't have at the moment, he thought frantically, along with his vision, movement, balance, and sense of direction.

Gregor did not respond to his question. Several miles later, after a bumpy ride, Hornberg felt himself violently flung to the left, as Gregor turned the big truck, until he was brought up short by his abductor's right arm. After another shorter distance, the truck came to a quick stop.

Hornberg heard another vehicle come to a stop adjacent to the one he was riding in. The passenger-side door was swung open, and he was assisted off the high truck seat by two men and escorted to the other waiting vehicle. Then, his senses told him, the new vehicle turned around and set off, one hundred-eighty degrees from his original course.

The vehicle drove down the sandy forest road at a high rate of speed, weaving only slightly to negotiate the occasional turns in the road. At last, Hornberg felt the vehicle turning right onto a hard asphalt road, or so the sound of the tires told him. This driver was silent, and after several miles, another hard right turn and a quick left turn brought them onto yet another bumpy dirt road.

Again, the vehicle quickly stopped. Another vehicle pulled adjacent, and the transfer was repeated. Hornberg's internal compass was now hopelessly disoriented; he no longer had any idea of where he might be in relation to his original abduction.

As they rattled down this new forest road, more slowly now, Gregor's voice addressed him. "Sorry about all the melodrama, Sidney, but we had to make sure that you weren't being followed. You can understand, I'm sure."

"Where are we going, Gregor?" Hornberg asked, in complete confusion.

"Soon enough, my friend," Gregor answered, in apparent sympathy. "For now, you should try to get some rest, we shall be traveling for perhaps another three-quarters of an hour yet."

After several more ninety-degree course changes, as it seemed to him in his sensory-deprived state, Hornberg felt the big truck slow and pull slowly off the road into what seemed to be a narrow two-track. He felt the truck's tires sliding in the snow into slippery, deep ruts as the truck cab rolled. Tree branches scratched loudly along both sides of the vehicle.

The truck made its way, painfully slowly, along the narrow path for a considerable distance. The bumping and scratching finally stopped, and they pulled into a level area. They waited there for a short time, and then another vehicle joined them.

After the vehicles were turned off, Hornberg's door was opened, and he was escorted by the two men, half-carried and half-dragged, across a slushy lawn. The men maneuvered him up several rows of steps and then through a heavy wooden door that creaked on its hinges. Hornberg momentarily flinched as a blast of warm air struck him in the face when the door was opened.

Hornberg was then seated on a rough wood plank bench at what felt like a picnic table. He heard the sharp sound of the lid of an old cast iron cook stove being lifted, the stirring sounds of coals being settled, and then the duller sound of wood on metal as more firewood was added. Gently, the duct tape that covered his eyes was cut by a shears and was worked off his head, even more gently where the hair of his head was attached to it. The duct tape binding his hands behind him was then cut and removed.

As Hornberg's eyes struggled to come into focus in the newly bright light and as he rubbed his wrists to massage some circulation into them, two figures came into view. Both men were clad in black and both wore ski masks, but one was a shorter, powerful-looking man and the other was tall and spare-framed. Little was discernible about either man except that they were both Caucasian, from what he could tell from the eyeholes of the masks and the wrists of their black formless shirts.

"So, Sidney, we meet at last!" said the taller of the two, with the little that Hornberg could see of his eyes crinkled in mirth, as if this were all some grand game.

"Indeed," said Hornberg, warily, as he picked small, sticky duct tape fragments from the hair of his head and neck and off his wrists. "I must say, Gregor," he continued, irritably, "you have gone to an awful lot of trouble to talk to me. You seem to know a lot about cell phones; was a simple telephone call too easy for your little game?"

"Unfortunately, Sidney, this is not a simple matter, and it is no game," said the tall man, now suddenly serious. "I think I know how you and your fellow Americans must feel. Probably the same way I might feel if someone had detonated an atomic device in my own country," Gregor continued. "I do feel badly that some of your citizens were unfortunately victims, but it can only underscore how serious we are about this matter."

Hornberg suddenly saw red. This condescending Slavic asshole wasn't any different than any of the other ruling classes of Europeans who had sent his Jewish ancestors into pogroms, or camps, or even worse, it seemed to him. He was probably a dead man anyway, he thought fatalistically, so what could it possibly matter?

"Shit or get off the pot, Gregor!" Hornberg replied, acidly. "If I could get to you right now across this table, if I knew that somehow I could keep you from killing any more innocent people in my country, I'd take you out with my fingers. Your ape there wouldn't be able to stop me before I'd choked your eyes out!" he said, spitting the words out while motioning to the short, powerful man next to Gregor. "Now just what the fuck do you want from me?" he asked, angrily.

The tall man chuckled softly. "Just as I've suspected all along, Sidney, you and I are cut from the same cloth," he replied gently. "It will not be necessary to choke me; I'll gladly tell you what you want to know. But first," he said, expansively, "let us be civilized."

Suddenly, a half-gallon fruit jar of clear liquid appeared on the table, along with three shot glasses. "A gift from our host," said Gregor, abstractly, with some apparent satisfaction. "Come, let us enjoy, so that we may have a more reasonable discussion."

Gregor quietly poured the clear liquid into the three glasses and then pushed one glass in front of each of them. Gregor and his companion each quickly drank theirs, and then they both looked to Hornberg. Oh, what the hell, thought Hornberg, and then he quickly downed his drink. As the alcohol exploded in his senses, a great sense of bliss enveloped him, an almost perverse sense of well-being under such life-threatening circumstances.

"Wonderful stuff," said Gregor, as to himself, with a distant look in his eyes. "We have nothing to compare to this where we are from." Then, pouring three more drinks into the glasses, he sat and faced Hornberg squarely.

"Tell me, Sidney," Gregor began abruptly, "have you ever heard of a Ukrainian physicist named Sergei Lysenko?"

Hornberg admitted that he had never heard the name. Then Gregor continued, in great detail: "Dr. Lysenko is well known in international scientific circles for his research into the manipulation of gravitational energy through the use of superconductors. His most recent papers, published in the former Soviet Union, describe an apparatus that generates a beam of pure gravitational energy."

Warming to his subject, Gregor went on: "The beam Doctor Lysenko describes supposedly is capable of exerting thousands of pounds of force on objects many kilometers away. It is apparently powerful enough to shatter brick, punch holes in concrete, and deform metal objects like hitting them with a sledgehammer," Gregor continued, pounding a fist on the wooden table to make his point. "Also, and most importantly, it is capable of penetrating materials and traveling long distances without any discernable loss of energy."

"A gravity beam?" Hornberg snorted derisively. "Sounds like science fiction hogwash to me."

"I might be inclined to agree, in your position, but my government would not," said Gregor, his gaze locked on Hornberg's face. "The good doctor has apparently found a way of focusing a high-energy discharge onto an yttrium-barium-copper oxide, superconducting ceramic disc, rotating in a magnetic field, and turning it into an impulse gravity generator." The words meant nothing to Hornberg.

In fact," Gregor continued excitedly, "apparently, the faster the object moves, the more force can be exerted on it, to the point of even vaporizing the target. The beam propagates at a very high speed, possibly light speed or greater, and its total force is proportional to target mass—in other words, exactly like gravity!" said the now passionate voice behind the mask.

"Think of it, Sidney!" Gregor continued enthusiastically, as Hornberg looked at him skeptically. "The ramifications are endless! Space transportation without rockets! Missile defense and gravity beam weapons! Electrical generation without fossil fuels or nuclear waste! Artificial gravity! And all of it immune to electromagnetic shielding of any kind! Mankind could be on the brink of eternal life!" Gregor enthused.

Hornberg was staggered. "I frankly don't know what to say," he admitted, confused.

"It is a lot to take in," Gregor replied, patiently, suddenly back in control again. "You and I are both basically military men, Sidney, and we do not have the imagination to be able to grasp such concepts readily. However," he continued assertively, "I assure you that many people in your own government take Dr. Lysenko's work completely seriously. In fact," he added, as if sharing a confidence, "your Boeing 'Phantom Works' in Seattle, Washington, which is probably the most secret research and development arm of your entire military-industrial complex, has been attempting to replicate his work for some time now, with all of it financed by your NASA organization."

Hornberg paused, thoughtfully, and then asked, "But what does that have to do with all of this?"

Gregor replied, carefully: "Doctor Lysenko disappeared from the Ukraine this past August. Your government kidnapped him. Boeing's work in Seattle is proof that they are still in correspondence with him today."

Hornberg was stunned. Slowly, revelation seemed to be parting the clouds of doubt that he had been immersed in for so long. "And?" he asked quizzically, prompting for an answer.

"And," continued Gregor, as if checking off mental boxes, "Doctor Lysenko entered the United States aboard an American merchant vessel at the port of Marquette at the end of August. There is no evidence that he ever left your Upper Peninsula. Doctor Lysenko has special needs," he added, "that make his trail extremely easy to follow. The trail leads here and ends here." His inference was immediately obvious to Hornberg

"It should be clear to you by now," Gregor continued pointedly, "that we want our scientist back. In absence of this," he said ominously, "we shall tear the heart out of your country and make its Midwest a polluted landscape, like Chernobyl in Ukraine, where no one lives!"

"Now drink up, Sidney," Gregor added, in a light tone, "for it is time for you to take another ride."

*　　*　　*　　*

Hornberg sat on the tall concrete step bundled in a sleeping bag, with his hands behind his back wrapped in duct tape and with a duct tape blindfold wrapped around his head. He had another headache, and the now familiar foul taste was again in his mouth.

Still, he thought, he wasn't particularly uncomfortable. His captors had made sure that his feet were dry, in woolen socks, and his head was in some sort of watch cap. These and the sleeping bag surrounding him gave him ample warmth.

After they had lifted him out of the truck cab onto the steps, 'Gregor' had slipped his cell phone back into his pocket before they had left in a shower of slushy snow and gravel, saying that he could "call a cab" soon, as daylight was on it's way. Hornberg could tell that he was near a hard road, for very occasionally a car passed by close at hand, close enough so that he could feel the wake of its passage. But for some time no one stopped, until at last he heard the sound of an old, wheezing vehicle pulling into the space in front of him.

"Wash the fuck are you shuppozed to be?" an inebriated voice called out to him through the rolled-down truck window.

"Excuse me, sir," Hornberg asked politely, "but you wouldn't happen to have a pocket knife on you, would you?"

Hornberg heard the old truck door creak open reluctantly. He felt his sleeping bag comforter being pulled down and the duct tape binding his hands being cut. As Hornberg pulled off the duct tape blindfold, his eyes slowly adjusted to the semi-gloaming that was illuminated by a big yard light.

Now that his vision had cleared, Hornberg saw that his rescuer was apparently a local person, dressed in a baseball cap and with flannel all over him. The man was driving an old black and red GMC pickup truck with a plow on the front. He could barely walk, Hornberg saw, the obvious victim of way too many beers.

Two other local 'wooly buggers' even more intoxicated than his benefactor peered at him from the old truck with black, beady eyes, like small owls in a tree cavity. As he glanced down the road, the glare of a small tavern across a small bridge told him instantly where his deliverance had come from in the early morning hours.

Glancing over his shoulder, Hornberg saw the rustic, hand-carved sign on the front the establishment, behind the steps that he had sat on: "*Paulding Store*', it said. Now, where the hell is Paulding, and where the hell am I, he wondered bemusedly?

CHAPTER 7

▼

Bill McCombs stood in the destruction of the aspen ridge, looking down on the big camp of his friend Carl Lemke. A few of the vehicles that had been parked in the big yard on his last trip here were no longer there. Despite the new snow and ideal tracking conditions, he had seen not a single human footprint in the creek bottom that ran out of Bob Lake, the area where he knew that the majority of Lemke's crew normally hunted.

Lemke's old truck and snowmobile trailer were still in the yard, but no smoke came from any of the chimney stovepipes on either the camp or the outbuildings. The yard itself was well trodden with human footprints and vehicle tracks, but the place seemed to be deserted, despite the cars still parked there.

Carefully and cautiously, McCombs made his way down the hill and flanked the camp, staying well back in the tree line out of sight. Sam, McCombs' springer spaniel, remained on the aspen ridge, poking into each of the many piles of slash and aspen debris with loud snorts and snuffles. The dog's tail was wagging so hard that it seemed as though it must eventually detach itself from the rest of his body. A good place for him, thought McCombs. There were more than enough nooks and crannies on the clear-cut ridge to keep the dog amused for hours.

As McCombs worked his way quietly behind the outbuilding that contained Lemke's still, he saw what appeared to be a brand-new Zodiac inflatable boat. The boat was twenty feet long, with twin one hundred twenty-five horsepower Yamaha outboards, on a trailer. It had been rolled backwards down the small ravine behind the building as if it had been discarded there. "Strange thing for a deer hunt," he muttered to himself quietly, beneath his breath.

McCombs carefully continued his quiet circle about the camp until he had completed a full three hundred sixty degrees. No footprints came and went through the trees in the new snow anywhere. Nobody at this camp was hunting, that seemed clear to McCombs.

Quietly approaching the front door of the camp, McCombs climbed the rough steps and knocked on the door. Only silence answered his knock. Depressing the rough latch, McCombs pushed the door inward, as it creaked on its hinges in protest.

The interior of the camp was dark and cold. On the table, a mostly full half-gallon fruit jar of clear liquid sat, along with three shot glasses. A chill shot through him, and the short hairs stood up on the back of his neck.

After backing out of the camp, McCombs climbed the hill towards the aspen ridge where he could see the springer spaniel digging frantically. Dirt and slushy snow sprayed up behind the dog as it worked a fair sized trench into the still soft ground at the edge of a large pile of slash. Coming up to the animal, McCombs could now see what the dog had found so attractive. A foot, a calf and a thigh, all encased in a long leather legging with sodden, gray woolen balls in a fringe about the top of it, protruded from the loosened soil at an odd angle.

*   *   *   *

The debriefing of Sidney Hornberg was still ongoing. Hornberg had been given a cursory physical, and aside from a lingering headache from the sedative that had been administered to him and a small cut on the back of his neck from his rough handling that was easily swabbed and bandaged, nothing wrong with him was obvious to the attending physician. His abductors had taken some care to avoid injuring him, that much was apparent.

The group in Hornberg's office had been going over and over his taped conversations with 'Gregor', searching for clues as to the man's identity and motivation. The considered opinion was still that he was somehow connected to either the Russian GRU or some other western European intelligence organization.

"I think that he's bluffing," said Colonel Wenzel to Wilton, the CIA man, referring to the taped threats to turn the Midwest into an American Chernobyl. "He knows that the man he's looking for is in the Upper Peninsula, so why ship his resources out to other places in the Midwest and risk a full retaliatory response from the United States if he detonates another device?"

"Doctor Lysenko?" asked Hornberg, in surprise. "He's here? In the Upper Peninsula?"

"Sergei Lysenko is a familiar name to us," Wilton replied, cryptically. "Doctor Lysenko is very well known in international scientific circles for his work on gravity."

Hornberg flushed red. "Goddammit, Wilton, just answer the question!" he demanded, acerbically. "You people snatched this Lysenko from the Ukraine and squirreled him away up here? This 'Star Wars' crap is what brought all of this down on our heads?" Hornberg demanded to know.

Just then, Hornberg's secretary buzzed his intercom. "Mr. Hornberg, Paul Adams on line one. He insisted that I break in on your meeting," she added apologetically.

Raising a cautioning hand to the others, Hornberg pushed the speaker connection. "Hey Paul, what's up?" he asked the Michigan State Police detective.

"Sorry to interrupt, Sid," Adams began, apologetically. "That must have been some ride you went on last night, but I've got a massacre on my hands here," he went on, grimly. "No shit!"

"What are you talking about, Paul?" Hornberg asked, as he glanced worriedly at the others in the room. "Where are you?"

"I'm three or four miles southeast of Rousseau in Ontonagon County, on a ridge behind a private hunting camp," Adams continued, breathing hard. "I've got eight victims in a shallow trench, all apparently middle-aged, white males. A local guy called it into the Ontonagon County Sheriff. Looks like they were all executed, all in the same way, single bullet in the back of the head. This is bad, Sid, it's a goddamn war zone out here!" The fear and excitement in Adams' voice was palpable.

"We're on our way, Paul!' yelled Hornberg into the speaker as he scrambled for his coat. The room erupted into a burst of activity, with all of the men trying to get through the door at the same time. "Give us directions on my cell phone when we get on the road!" Hornberg shouted, over his shoulder.

*   *   *   *

Hornberg's car bumped its way down the narrow two-track, slipping and sliding into deep ruts, with tree branches deeply scratching the paint of the car for the length of its carefully washed government exterior. Finally, they pulled into a large yard that surrounded a big hunting camp. Over thirty other vehicles were already present, including three ambulances.

Hornberg and his passengers, Wilton and Wenzel, could see that the ridge behind the camp was frenetic with activity. Figures scrambled everywhere, running yellow tape and carefully examining every square inch of the denuded clear-cut. Hornberg could see the large outline of Adams off to one side beside a large pile of slash, with several county officials and a rough-cut figure in woods clothes. He left his car and headed up the ridge towards the detective, with the others in tow.

Gaining the top of the ridge, Hornberg and the others saw Adams standing at one end of a procession of body bags, eight in all. The bags were lying next to each other at the edge of a hastily excavated trench that was perhaps three feet deep.

Kneeling at the first of the bags, Hornberg zipped it part way down to gaze at of the face of the man inside; a face that was dirty and contorted, in the all-too-familiar fashion of a man who had been in the ground for some time. Zipping the bag back up, kneeling at the second bag, and then repeating the process, Hornberg saw the same result; another dirty, dead face, like so many of the other faces that he had seen in his life.

God, thought Hornberg, mournfully, almost as if praying to an entity that he had long since dismissed as being irrelevant in the callous world that he, Hornberg, inhabited, am I never going to stop having to look at dead bodies? What could these poor bastards have done to deserve this? But no answer came to him.

"They're all the same, Sid," said Adams, sadly. "Looks like they all died at the same time and then got quickly buried up here—had some of this aspen slash pulled over the trench to conceal it a little. If it hadn't have been for Mr. McCombs, here," he said, motioning to the civilian next to him, who stood out from the others by his rough clothing, "they could have been here for a very long time, once the ground froze and we got some significant snow, before anybody found them."

"Do we know who they were?" Hornberg asked, gazing once more with compassion at the cold face on the ground at his feet before zipping up the body bag again.

"Well, we haven't had time to call in any prints or DNA yet, but yeah, they all had I.D. on them," Adams replied. "Also, Mr. McCombs has identified several of them for us. He had known them for a few years, apparently. This camp was owned by a Carl Lemke, he tells us, from Pontiac, and he and this same crew came up every year for rifle season."

"Mr. McCombs," asked Hornberg, compassionately, addressing the civilian, "how is it that you found this?"

"Actually, my dog found them," McCombs replied, in gulps, as if gasping for air. "Carl Lemke was my friend!" added McCombs, his face tortured, with tears running from his eyes. "I was here four days ago, and there were people here then, but there was nobody that I recognized from a distance."

"What kind of animals are the people who did this?" McCombs emoted. "If I had followed my instincts then," he added, morosely, "maybe my friend would be alive today!"

"I wouldn't be so hard on myself, Mr. McCombs," Hornberg told him gently. "You could very well have been dead yourself by now if you had looked more closely then. And, from what I can see, the men in these bags have been dead for longer than four days," he told the grieving man.

"And you are correct; the men who killed these people are animals!" Hornberg said, solemnly, as the black-masked vision of 'Gregor' formed in his mind's eye. "We will do everything in our power to find them for you. And for your friend," he added compassionately

"There's some interesting things in the camp, Sid," said Adams, softly, with a nod to Wilton and Wenzel. "You might want to check it out, there's nothing much you can do up here. Start with that outbuilding by the ravine," he added cryptically.

Hornberg headed down the ridge, followed by Wilton and Wenzel, slipping and sliding in the slushy snow. As they approached the outbuilding, they noticed the Zodiac on the trailer pushed backwards into the ravine.

"So that's how they smuggled the big boom-booms in," said Wilton to the others. "Brought them in on the *Kharkiv*, ran out to collect them, and then left us a little going-away present."

"Looks that way," agreed Hornberg. "Well, we'll run the serial numbers of the boat, outboards, and trailer and see what comes up, but I doubt we'll find much other than that some guy paid cash for them at a Detroit boat show."

The men glanced quickly through the door of the outbuilding with some interest at the distilling apparatus inside, but the smell of the various tubs and buckets of corn mash, in differing states of decay and fermentation, was too overpowering. Nothing too unusual about this, Hornberg thought. Paul Adams had told him many tales, over the years, of the various illicit activities that took place during the Upper Peninsula deer rifle season. Almost all of it was usually treated with a wink and a knowing look by the local authorities. The rifle season was simply too important to the local economy to get overly concerned about normal human failings, he'd been told.

Walking to the front of the large camp, they climbed the rough steps together. Hornberg pushed on the door after depressing the rudimentary latch, and the door swung inward on its hinges, creaking in protest.

Although now dark and cold, the scene that came into view was immediately familiar to Hornberg, who had last seen it when the room was brightly lit and warm. The picnic table stood in the middle of the room in front of the cast-iron cook stove, surrounded by rude wooden benches. The half-gallon fruit jar that was still mostly full of clear liquid and the three shot glasses sat in the middle of the table, exactly as he remembered them.

He had sat, Hornberg recalled vividly, precisely in this same spot on the previous night, having a drink and a conversation with 'Gregor' and his companion, as the bodies of eight innocent men lay chilling in the ground on the ridge behind the camp. The room swirled. Running outside to the porch, Hornberg grasped the railing for support and vomited profusely, his body contorted in spasms with the effort.

CHAPTER 8

▼

The young President of the United States sat in the darkened room in the west end of the White House in Washington, D.C., flanked by his closest group of advisors and a select few others. The Vice-President and the Secretaries of State and Defense were present; as were the National Security Advisor, the Directors of the CIA and the FBI, the Attorney General, and several senior military officers from the Pentagon, Including the Chairman of the Joint Chiefs of Staff. The President's Press Secretary and his chief political officer were also present, but they sat well in the background, out of sight and out of mind.

The room was lit only by a roaring fire in the fireplace at the far end of the room and by the dim light of communications equipment. The President and his advisors sat in the dark mahogany furniture that was scattered about the room, silently contemplating their various competing priorities.

The President much preferred these closed, comfortable meetings, meetings that were somewhat like his 'Skull and Crossbones' days at Yale University, than with the usual open discussion at staff meetings and briefings. The annoying press constantly threw uncomfortable questions at him at briefings, and they seemed to always stray from the script that had been provided to them by his press secretary. The English language, and the constant 'put-and-take', had never been his forte.

No, the President felt much more comfortable here, in these White House surroundings, in this quiet, private antechamber. His father, who had served as President before him, had also preferred this room, where much of the behind-the-scenes planning for the first invasion of Iraq, 'Operation Desert Storm', had taken place.

The young President, buoyed by an anemic thirty thousand-vote majority in the closest U.S. presidential election in history, had decided to his satisfaction that he had somehow been given a mandate to decide the course of the world for the next fifty years. The almost immediate attack by the terrorists on the New York City Twin Towers and the Pentagon following his election had only strengthened this conviction and had given him an almost messianic view of his role in the world.

Since then, success had since followed success, as the rag-tag, pretentious Islamic Fundamentalists of Afghanistan, the Taliban, had been blasted into non-existence by the might of the United States armed forces. After their demise, the Taliban's terrorist sponsors and the perpetrators of 9/11, Al Queda, had burrowed into the deepest holes available along the Afghan-Pakistani border and were currently defying all efforts to dig them out. Soon enough, though, the President thought, soon enough!

The young Commander-In-Chief saw himself as a wartime President, involved in a titanic struggle with forces of evil all over the world. He frequently fantasized of stepping down from the cockpit of a fighter plane after having led his forces into victory, flight suit on and helmet in hand, as his own father had done so many wars ago. "Mission accomplished!" the banners would proclaim, as he was greeted by adoring crowds.

But it was not enough, his political advisors had told him, to proclaim the nation involved in a fight to the death with some faceless enemy, in remote places all over the globe. No, they had said, with his reelection coming up in two years it was necessary to put a name and a face to the enemy, some known evil entity, a country that could actually be seen as having been vanquished, in justifiable retribution, going into the campaign. And what better country than Iraq, they had advised; a country sitting astride twenty percent of the world's known oil reserves, one led by a murderous, corrupt regime, in a part of the world that had never known democracy?

The President had never thought of himself as a deep thinker, but rather as a leader; a leader who was guided by a deeply moral compass, who knew instinctively what the right thing to do was and who stuck to his first impressions despite any efforts by critics to dissuade him. His gut instincts had served him well for his entire political life, and he was sticking to them again.

No, the coming military campaign against Iraq was a certainty, the President knew in his heart. It was simply a matter of his staff coming up with sufficient justification for the war. His advisors had assured him that the need for war was self-evident to most of the world, but justification was still needed to persuade weak-kneed allies, such as Germany and France, to join his 'Grand Coalition'. This coalition would not only share the economic and military burden of the attack, but it would also share the inevitable spoils of victory, Iraqi oil and the lucrative contracts for the rebuilding of that country's infrastructure.

There would be no second chance for Iraq this time, the President had decided, like the one created by the debacle that had followed Desert Storm in 1991. Then, a coalition of nations led by the United States had ejected the invading Iraqi army from Kuwait but had fallen apart within view of Baghdad, leaving the same murderous regime in power. That debacle, the President reminded himself constantly, had been largely responsible for the subsequent failure of his own father's reelection campaign.

No, thought the President, momentarily alone with his thoughts in the darkened room, invading Iraq was clearly the right thing to do. It would be a cakewalk, his advisors had assured him, and his victorious troops would be greeted with "flowers in the streets" as they marched down the Baghdad boulevards, with Saddam Hussein dead and gone.

The timing was perfect, the President firmly believed. The new Russian Federation was too fragmented and too preoccupied with its own internal strife to do anything other than object to American movements in the Middle East. And so what if Germany and France were acting like nervous grandmothers chaperoning a stag party, he thought disdainfully. After all, they had been in bed with Saddam ever since Desert Storm. If they didn't come along, they'd be left out afterwards. The United States could easily go it alone, the President had concluded, with help from Great Britain and from the grateful Kuwaitis and Saudis.

The President glanced quickly around the room at his advisors. He thought of them not as personalities in their own right, each with their own duties to the Executive Branch of the government, but simply as supporting players in the advancement of his administration's agenda. He assessed each of them quickly, in small, thumbnail mental sketches as was his habit, for the value that each brought to his administration and to the upcoming Iraq campaign.

The Vice-President was a man who was sick and dour most of the time. However, as the President knew well, he was also tied in at the very highest levels with the U.S. military-industrial complex. That industrial powerhouse would be needed to quickly to fill the vacuum created by the collapsed Iraqi infrastructure, which would necessarily be bombed out of existence during the coming invasion. Quickly rebuilding Iraq and installing a government friendly towards the United States, before neighboring Iran was able to fill the void, was seen by the President as imperative, to ensure American domination of the post-war Middle East region and continued access to its oil reserves.

The Secretary of Defense and the CIA Director were the cheerleaders for the planned invasion. They were both take-charge, "take no prisoners" sorts of advocates who invigorated the President. They had long ago convinced him that any unintended consequences of the upcoming military operation would sort themselves out later, as these things always did.

His National Security Advisor was a woman possessed of both a sharp intelligence and a driving ambition. She was a tower of personal support for the President, and she also owed her career to him. It was uncanny, the President often thought, how it was that her opinions and advice exactly mirrored his own thinking.

The Attorney General, it seemed to the President, always looked as if he had gas as he struggled with the legal niceties that were necessary to implement the President's strategy for the War on Terror. By the new rules that his administration was making up as it went along, this war would require the curtailment of civil liberties and freedom of information, and the dismissal of the Geneva Convention provisions concerning the treatment of prisoners; draconian measures that were necessary to provide the secrecy and the intelligence to fight this new kind of war. However, the Attorney General was also a team player, the President knew, and he would do whatever was necessary, even if he gave himself an ulcer in the process.

Of all of his advisors, only the Secretary of State truly concerned the President. A retired four-star Army General who had served as the Chairman of the Joint Chiefs of Staff for his father during Desert Storm, the diplomat was highly respected, both in and out of the military, at home and internationally.

In the President's view, the Secretary of State sometimes acted as if he alone actually understood that the costs, both human and economic, of the proposed course of action in Iraq, and that they might be greater than the country would be willing to bear. The Secretary, alone among the President's closest advisors, seemed to agonize in their private discussions about the proposed invasion and the purported reasons for it, and he appeared as if he desperately wanting to say something to oppose it.

But at the same time, the Secretary of State had been a professional military man who had risen to the highest rank, one who had learned early in his career that it was never wise to question the judgment of his superiors. And so, now the President was treated almost daily to television images of his Secretary of State enumerating to the world the reasons that the invasion of Iraq was necessary, with facial and body expressions that connoted that he didn't quite believe those same reasons himself. Too late now to change horses, the President thought, but things would damn sure change at the beginning of his next term!

Here they were, thought the President in the darkened room, with all these irons in the fire, and he was supposed to worry about some piss-ant problem way up north in Michigan! Some place called 'Ontonagon' or some name like that; he wasn't even sure where this place was. The President hated to have to deal with details. That's why he had a Cabinet, he felt; his job was to think Big Picture.

"So, Stan, remind me again why we're talking about this Michigan thing," the President asked the Director of the FBI.

"Well, Mr. President, if you'll recall, it was a small atomic explosion in United States waters, and it sunk a Ukrainian-flagged ship," the FBI man replied, carefully.

"Yeah, but I was told that it didn't do much more than that but rattle the windows in that village up there," the President recalled. He didn't really understand what the big deal was.

The concept of an atomic explosion was only a vague abstraction to the young Commander-In-Chief. It was a tool that he knew he always had at his disposal, since the military man with the 'football' followed him everywhere. But, he had never personally witnessed such an explosion. The president had dismissed the use of such weapons, at least in his mind, as irrelevant in this new age, when there were no impending nuclear confrontations with threatening superpowers. The physics and implications of such a blast were foreign to his thinking, they having been absent from his Yale curriculum. He had been far too young to be any more than peripherally involved in the Cold War nuclear politics of his father's time in office.

"Correct, Mr. President, but in this case it appears that there may have been some Russian, or at least western European, involvement in this," the CIA Director chimed in. "There have since been additional civilian deaths up there that are also apparently connected to the case but are not related to the actual explosion. Additionally, the group believed to be responsible claims to have more nuclear devices in this country."

"Russian involvement? Are you sure?" asked the President, surprised. He had just had the new President of the Russian Federation, a man even younger than himself, as a guest at his Texas ranch. 'The V-Man', as the President thought of him, given his penchant for giving nicknames to acquaintances so that he wouldn't have to remember and pronounce their names, hadn't seemed to be the bellicose warrior type to him.

A small, nervous fellow, the Russian had seemed to the President to be completely consumed with the turmoil in his own country, a man who saw conspiracy and treachery everywhere. Which is exactly the way the President wanted to keep him, if possible, since Russian interference in the current activities of the United States in the Middle East was obviously unacceptable.

"Well, Mr. President," said the CIA Director, "we can't be completely certain, of course, but information obtained by our operatives," he continued, with a nod towards the FBI director and the Joint Chiefs Chairman, "seems to point to involvement by the Russian GRU, possibly using nuclear artillery shells that went missing from a Russian storage facility in 1998."

"That hardly seems possible," replied the President, as if in disbelief. "The Russian President has assured me that their nuclear weapons storage security is air-tight."

"He may have been overstating things a bit, Mr. President," continued the CIA Director, carefully. "The Russians have over twenty thousand of these small tactical devices stored all over their country. We don't know exactly how many, and maybe the Russians don't either."

We do know conclusively," the CIA Director continued, matter-of-factly, "that at least some of these smaller tactical nuclear weapons went missing or were stolen following the break-up of the Soviet Union, when these devices were removed from the former republics back to Russia for storage. Where they are now, no one knows. It is very possible, and quite probable, given our information," he added, with another nod at the FBI Director, "that the devices that may be in Michigan at the present were part of this small fraction that was somehow lost."

"Terrorists?" asked the President, tersely. "That Al-Queda bunch? I thought we had all of those rag-heads bottled up in Afghanistan!"

"Possibly, Sir, but not likely," replied the CIA Director, earnestly, with a slow shake of his head. "We think that this has all the earmarks of a Russian Special Forces operation. Our people on the scene seem to agree. Of course, it easily could be another country in the region as well, Ukraine for example, but it would still have to have the tacit support of Russia."

"But why would the Russians bother with such a piss-ant little weapon?" the President asked, perplexed. "They've still got tons of their big strategic warheads if they wanted to nuke us!"

"And so do we, Mr. President," interjected the Joint Chiefs Chairman. "It's the same old Mexican standoff," he added, with a shrug, "'Mutually Assured Destruction'. Russia, or China, or any of the other powers that possess nuclear weapons, know that they'll get it back twice as bad as we do if they ever launch against us!" he enthused with grim satisfaction, a steely glint in his eyes.

"Using a small tactical device like this has several advantages for them, in our view, Mr. President," contributed the Secretary of Defense, squinting at the Commander-in-Chief through his thick glasses with his head slightly tilted, like a small myopic hawk. "First, it's very portable, and it is almost impossible to find until it's too late. Second," he added, "it gives them deniability, since many more nations have tactical nukes than have strategic nukes."

"Third, Sir," added his National Security Advisor, trying carefully to gauge what the President would want to hear, "they may be trying to come in under the radar, by using a small enough device to have the desired effect without provoking a full nuclear retaliatory response from us."

"My God!" said the President, in astonishment. "That's pretty goddamn clever! They can run around our country with a truck full of small nuclear bombs, and we can't find them, stop them or pin it on them! And unless we're willing to blow up most of the world, we can't pay them back in kind! I didn't think that the 'V-Man' had it in him!" he added, in grudging admiration.

"Mr. President, it is quite possible that your Russian counterpart knows nothing about this," replied the Secretary of State, thoughtfully, as he recalled his years of military experience in dealings with the Soviets during the Cold War. "The Russian GRU operates pretty much independently from the Russian civilian government," he went on to say, "and they report only to the Defense Minister and the Chief of General Staff, both of whom are old, hard-line Communists from the Khrushchev era. They don't routinely share information or projects with anybody, other than between themselves. This could either be a full-blown GRU operation," he added, pensively, "or it could be some rogue GRU splinter faction, with its own particular axe to grind."

"So do we know what they're after?" asked the President, returning his gaze to the CIA Director.

"Well, Sir," the CIA man replied, "there's been some communication between our operatives and this group about gravity research conducted by a Ukrainian physicist named Sergei Lysenko; research that apparently has some fantastic implications."

"'Star Wars' stuff?" asked the President, derisively.

"No, Sir, Mr. President!" replied the Joint Chiefs Chairman, enthusiastically. "This is 'Operation Thunderbolt,' a project that you were first briefed on last month."

"When Doctor Lysenko first conducted this gravity research in Russia," the Secretary of Defense explained, "he apparently had to use some kind of massive laboratory voltage generator that was capable of generating about five million volts," he recalled, from his briefing papers on the project. "Completely impractical from other than an experimental viewpoint, of course," added the Secretary. The President vaguely remembered the briefing now.

"Unfortunately," continued the Defense Secretary, "the Russians have apparently gotten wind somehow of the fact that the Boeing 'phantom works' in Seattle, through manipulation of the composition of the ceramic materials involved using their Cray supercomputer, have gotten the necessary voltages down to the twenty-thousand volt range, well within the capabilities of most standard industrial electrical generating equipment. Our initial experiments to date look quite promising."

The President clearly remembered the details now. The perfect anti-missile defense, he'd been told, a defense that had been sought by every American President since the end of World War II, might be within his grasp, and further ramifications almost beyond belief might follow that. Well, the young Commander-in-Chief instantly decided, this would be one genie that wasn't going to get out of the bottle, at least not on his watch!

"We certainly aren't going to let them have 'Operation Thunderbolt', that's not even negotiable!" the President stated, in no uncertain terms. "Stan and Bob," he ordered, addressing the FBI and CIA directors, "you had better start kicking some ass up there in Ontonagon or wherever the hell that godforsaken place is, get some boots on the ground and find these assholes! Get the Joint Chiefs to give you some troops, if that's what you need!" he added for emphasis, nodding towards that senior officer. The President loved military jargon, and he practiced it all the time. He tried to interject it wherever he could, as a proper Commander-In-Chief should.

"Well, Sir, it doesn't appear that the issue for the Russians is the Boeing work, from what our operatives tell us," the CIA Director replied, uncomfortably. "It seems as though they want their man back."

"Man? What man? Who are we talking about here?" demanded the President.

"Doctor Sergei Lysenko, Mr. President," replied the CIA Director, in a muted voice. "We have had him in isolation in Michigan's Upper Peninsula since last August. He's the man behind the Operation Thunderbolt work that you've been briefed on."

"Lysenko?" asked the President, wide-eyed. "We have him? We rescued him?"

"'Rescued' is a bit overstated, Sir," continued the CIA Director, carefully. "Actually, we took him. It was never intended that the Russians would know that we have him."

"And so," said the President, the situation finally becoming clear to him, "it's probably not a coincidence that they set this atom bomb off up there, is it?"

"No, Sir," replied his National Security Advisor, with a thoughtful look on her face. "We think that they are sending us a very clear message."

CHAPTER 9

▼

The dream, or some close version, was always the same. He, a mere mortal, had somehow become an assistant to *Nanabohzo*, the guardian of man and a spirit. *Nanabohzo* had been born on a great island at the eastern end of Lake Superior, the first son of an Ojibwa spirit-god and his human wife. He, the man, attended to and assisted his god-like master as he roamed the world and brought to mankind all of its present gifts and abilities, sometimes by accident and sometimes not.

Nanabozho spoke with all living creatures, and he could transform himself into any of them, as he wished. He was the ultimate trickster, but he was also benevolent at the same time. He both bestowed and he took away, as his dual spirit-human personality and whims dictated. In his godly guise, he gave the porcupine his quills, so that it could better protect itself from the bears, the wolves, and the fishers that wished to eat it. And yet, he also took away the power of speech from the animals, because they had conspired against humankind.

Nanabozho ruled the earth. He covered it with snow and ice in the winter, locking tight its lakes and streams, when he was displeased with his human offspring. And then, he covered it in green and spring blooms, after he had relented and had forgiven them. He brought his children the first fire by transforming himself into a humble rabbit, in order to sneak into the wigwam of the Firekeeper in order to hide burning coals in his fur. To this day, the coat of the snowshoe hare turns brown in the summer in memory of this great gift. Among his Ojibwa children, *Nanabozho* is still called 'The Great Rabbit' accordingly.

Nanabozho would occasionally show his human side as well. He made mistakes like humans did, but he never seemed to learn from them. More telling, he always wanted to believe in the basic goodness of his human children, but he was invariably disappointed.

Nanabozho killed fierce animals that threatened his human children. The old white bones that are found now by paleontologists are the remains of those creatures that he slew, long ago. He taught the people how to make arrow points and spears, hatchets. and canoes. He showed them how to cultivate corn, beans, and squash. And, after he had watched a spider catching flies, he taught his children how to make nets to catch fish.

Nanabozho taught the people about maple sugar and how to make it; the sticky confection was the only spice that the Ojibwa ever knew before the coming of the white man, and it was used on every kind of food. He showed them how to picture-write on rocks, and where places were to find herbs to use as medicine, places that are still marked with small offerings by The People when they come upon them.

In his dream, he, the man, followed his master as he traveled throughout the world, and witnessed his great deeds. And, as they marked each day's journey with a pile of stones, the stones would become the rocky promontories and mountains of these far northern lands.

Nanabozho's footprints are still everywhere today in this country, in every strangely formed rock along every cataract that hurtles towards *Ke-che-gum-me*, the Great Water. Once, when the man had watched *Nanabozho* dam a river to catch beaver, the dirt that he had thrown out had become the Apostle Islands. And then, when they had rested beside another pleasant stream, the imprints of *Nanabohzo*'s heels, elbows, and his great body had become the perfectly smooth boreholes in the sandstone banks of the Presque Isle River, near its confluence with Lake Superior.

Each of the man's dreams, however, always seemed to end in the same way: a final titanic struggle between his master, *Nanabozho*, and the Evil One, in this northern place, with he, the man, as a helpless bystander. At stake was always the future of humankind; for, should *Nanabozho* be vanquished, the Earth would surely burst into flames, and all living creatures would be destroyed.

At this point, invariably, the dream would end, as Agent Thomas Loonsfoot woke up, almost automatically, some few minutes before the physicist in his charge would rouse himself for his daily routine. As the mental fog cleared and as Loonsfoot became aware of his surroundings, the low red light of the bunker would illuminate row upon row of transformers, power supplies, inverters and scientific instruments, stacked on top of each other neatly, on shelves beyond the open door to his sleeping area. Each piece of equipment was dotted with colored status lights, and each displayed a myriad of gauges and pointers with backlit scales.

A low background hum seemed to permeate the whole place, from the instruments and from the heating and air conditioning, although after all this time Loonsfoot was no longer consciously aware of it. This must be what life is like for sailors on a submarine that was submerged in the ocean, he had thought many times; except that he was submerged in a wooded hillside, beneath old trees.

Although it was subdued, the red light provided more than sufficient illumination for the interior of the bunker. Loonsfoot had come to actually prefer it to normal white light, for it was much easier on the eyes. For the physicist, it was an absolute necessity, due to his medical condition. Even with the red light, many of the apparatuses and equipment had off-lit lighting and other special optical devices to make them easier for the scientist to use.

Loonsfoot and the physicist were the only full time occupants of the bunker. Every four days, a small crew of three civilians contracted to the Agency, who performed maintenance, cleaned, and cooked meals, relieved their previous counterparts. They would then settle into small anterooms off from the main bunker for their four-day stint of caring for and supporting the scientist.

Loonsfoot watched the crews come and go. He interacted with them only to the extent of giving necessary instructions and taking his meals. It had been made very clear to him by his CIA superiors that this was a highly secret project, and that no fraternization was permitted.

Loonsfoot continuously marveled at the ingenuity that the Agency had displayed in concealing the large bunker complex. Located within the eighteen thousand acre Sylvania Wilderness Area in the Ottawa National Forest, a few miles southwest of the town of Watersmeet, the bunker sat directly below what was purported to be a scientific research project called the 'Helen Lake Flux Tower'. The flux tower area, at the end of a nondescript two track behind a locked gate by a small lake of the same name, was supposedly an environmental research project that was funded by the Department of Energy. Only a select few knew that this was a clever CIA cover story.

Located on high ground, in a stand of old growth hardwoods and softwoods ranging in age up to three hundred fifty years, the site was described for public consumption as being designed to "measure the ecosystem exchange between the old trees and their surroundings and to measure the trees' growth, as influenced by climate variability". This explanation neatly explained the power supplies running into the site from the nearest county road, the beaten-down ruts, and the nearly constant barrage of visitors through the locked gate on the busy two-track. The perfect cover for a covert scientific project, thought Loonsfoot, admiringly.

The occasional casual visitor to the site saw only the above-ground power supplies, the thirty-seven meter high flux tower, and the various enclosures that housed scientific instruments. Different kinds of sensors were attached to nearly every tree in the area. Probes were stuck into the ground in many different places. Wires and tubing ran everywhere, like some sort of manic high school science project run amuck in the middle of the forest.

The most frequent visitors, the researchers and the graduate students from the University of Minnesota and Penn State, had beaten paths into the ground as they made their way between their instruments and the flux tower collecting data. Not visible to any visitor was the fully equipped, state of the art, scientific research facility that was contained within the bunker beneath the tower, some twenty feet below the old trees.

The entrance to the bunker was on a steep slope that fell away down to the shore of a small bay of Helen Lake. One entered through a power-operated door on a hydraulic slide. The door was carefully camou-flaged to blend into the hillside itself, in a manner such that only the clos-est examination would reveal it.

The pale physicist, naturally curious, had discovered the door's operat-ing mechanism a mere twenty minutes after first having been moved into the bunker in the dead of night, during his first inquisitive, cursory explo-ration of his new surroundings. He had opened and closed the clever door, both from inside the bunker and from outside at the controller hidden in an old hemlock stump, for hours, fascinated, to the point that the operat-ing mechanism's hydraulic seals had begun to leak and had needed to be replaced.

The bunker itself was spacious. It contained ample living and sleeping areas for the scientist and for his research materials, books, and computers. It also easily contained the many tons of power supplies and heating and ventilating equipment, and the cooking facilities, toilets, showers, and quarters for Loonsfoot and for the support staff.

The entire bunker was climate controlled. It was maintained at a con-stant temperature and humidity, for comfort and to protect the many del-icate scientific instruments. Meals prepared within the bunker by the three-man crew were good, balanced, and varied. Nothing but the best for 'The Package', as Loonsfoot had at first heard described the pale Ukrainian physicist now under his charge.

The back end of the bunker terminated into what Loonsfoot thought of as the 'shooting gallery'; a long, straight, horizontal borehole several hun-dred yards deep that was serviced by a small mechanical track. The track was controlled by hydraulics, and on it the scientist attached his ceramic discs, targets, and other devices. An imposing array of focusing devices, the purpose of which Loonsfoot had little idea of other than that they were apparently all powered by one or more of the many power supplies and inverters lining the length of the bunker, were mounted on portable carts at the other end of the borehole. A bank of several different computer ter-minals and keyboards were mounted along the wall on one side.

The pale scientist spent most of his working hours at this end of the bunker. He appeared almost transparent, with his pale skin and hair, in the low red light, while he was taking careful notes on a small clipboard, performing calculations, sitting at one of the computer terminals while inputting data, or adjusting one or more of the focusing devices at some unseen target somewhere down the borehole.

Occasionally, while he casually observed the scientist, Loonsfoot would be rewarded with a sharp report and a brief flash of light from somewhere down the borehole, after which the physicist would furiously scribble notes and then retreat to one of the computer keyboards. Of what these events signified, he had no idea.

The physicist's nightly excursions had come about almost naturally, for he had never lost his fascination with the clever hydraulic door at the entrance to the bunker. One night, after having opened the door and leaving the bunker, he had simply kept on walking.

Loonsfoot had followed the pale man, keeping him in view but making no attempt to restrain him in any way, since he was under no instructions to do so. And so it had been ever since, with the tacit approval of Loonsfoot's CIA superiors. They not only trusted Loonsfoot's instincts and knowledge of the terrain, but they also knew that 'The Package' would be much more cooperative and amenable with regular exercise, in this last true wilderness area of the entire Great Lakes region.

It had become a regular routine. The scientist, who never slept more than a few hours at most, would awaken, perform his morning hygiene, eat breakfast, and then work furiously until lunch. After lunch, he would again work furiously until dinner. After dinner, he would nap until sunset. Then he would rise, snack on whatever was handy, and then head out into the woods once it was truly dark, unless the weather was particularly inclement. Loonsfoot could almost set his watch by him.

Always, Agent Thomas Loonsfoot would follow a respectful thirty paces or so behind the scientist, to give him his space. He would watch the Ukrainian scientist, in his odd, genetically malformed body, as he wandered the forest, looking about him in abject wonder; the same forest that he, Loonsfoot, had known so intimately, for so many years, that he no longer truly saw it anymore, at least in the same way that the physicist did.

Loonsfoot took in the pale man's childish delight in each small discovery. He saw his charge's amazement at the sights of the creatures of the night and the predators that hunt them. He marveled at the man's careful attention to the sounds of tiny watercourses tinkling their way over smooth stones before quietly sliding into silence in the mosses of the bogs, and the slaps of beavers' tails on the surfaces of their small, carefully crafted ponds, and the louder splashes of the smallmouth bass pursuing their nightly prey on the mirrored surfaces of the Sylvania's bigger lakes.

As he watched the pale man, Loonsfoot found himself looking back in time, to his own youth, as he saw the man living out his delayed childhood, a childhood that apparently had been denied to him through some gross injustice. His charge, this 'Package', was as different from himself as, literally, dusky brown to translucent white; but for all of that, he empathized with the pale Ukrainian.

Loonsfoot eventually became aware that he had become as much a captive of the albino Ukrainian physicist as the scientist was of him. And at the end of the nightly excursion, when they had retreated to the red-lit confines of the bunker, both were satiated, from the experience and from the emotion. Their unspoken bond grew stronger every day.

Loonsfoot knew that he had somehow been unconsciously transcended, like his Ojibwa Bear Clan ancestors, from not just a 'watcher' but to a 'protector' of the exiled physicist. He had begun to look after the pale man as if he had been his own child; a child whose language and actions he couldn't begin to understand, but no longer simply as at the beginning, when the Ukrainian had first come to the bunker. The two still did not speak much, since they could barely understand each other. But, both seemed to know that they had managed to assimilate some small part of the other, and that they were communicating in an unspoken way.

Loonsfoot had become fiercely protective of the scientist, almost to the dismay of his CIA superiors, who were correctly concerned that he was beginning to lose his objectivity. One night, when the two had traveled too far from the bunker to be able to return by sunrise, far to the south of

Clark Lake, Loonsfoot had simply had the man lie in a high, dry depression. There he had covered him with leaves and other litter from the forest floor. As the physicist slept through the daylight hours, comfortable in his dark cocoon, Loonsfoot had sat guard at his head like some great Ojibwa sphinx, alert and sleepless for many hours.

When they had returned to the bunker the next evening, the remonstrations from Loonsfoot's CIA superiors had been loud and resounding. Thoroughly chastened, Loonsfoot had afterwards ensured that the scientist always shortened his nightly forays considerably.

In late September, Loonsfoot had persuaded a cousin from Watersmeet to bring a small aluminum canoe to the Clark Lake day use area and beach. Loonsfoot and the Ukrainian had found the canoe where it had been left. Together, they had carried it to a high spot between a trio of small ponds due south of the bunker called, whimsically, 'Louise', 'Dorothy', and 'Elsie'; far from the prying eyes of the U.S. Forest Service that jealously guarded the more popular of the Wilderness' bigger lakes.

After that, their nightly trips, while the pleasant fall weather held, had typically been to put the canoe on one of these small water bodies. Loonsfoot would be in the back, manning the paddle, while the luminous scientist lounged in the bow. The pale man's features would be set alight by the faint glow of the stars as the man, with his pale fingers sometimes trailing in the water, followed the stars' journeys across the heavens and listened carefully for the night sounds of the beaver, and the woodcock, geese, and ducks that were beginning their yearly migrations to the south.

Now, however, the weather had grown cold. The beavers were silent, and the migratory birds were gone. The small ponds were frozen, and the canoe lay concealed in a stand of small evergreens, awaiting the spring.

Their nightly excursions had been reduced to the area directly around the bunker, where their tracks in the snow blended in with those of the many scientific visitors to the above-ground research facility. Their time out of the bunker was both short in length and exceedingly cautious, with Loonsfoot staying closer to the physicist than he ever had before. The scientist had not been told of the reason for Loonsfoot's heightened alertness, but he could sense the tension in his taciturn Indian companion, and he silently wondered about it.

Loonsfoot now knew about the nature of the explosion that the two had observed from the tower. He knew that men, foreign men and ruthless killers, were searching for the pale physicist in his charge. He knew about the sinking of the *Kharkiv* and the slaying of the Rousseau hunters, and his normal, cautious Indian nature now verged on full-blown paranoia.

Loonsfoot took no further time off to go to Watersmeet to visit friends and family. Nothing now escaped his attention; he carefully monitored each routine shift change for a face or an action that seemed out of place. And yet, each night the dream would return to him in his sleep, with each night's dream more vivid than the night before; and each day began with a dull sense of foreboding.

CHAPTER 10

▼

The old man known as winter arrives almost unnoticed in Michigan's Upper Peninsula. He slowly enters the scene on his ancient, crippled feet, with his back stooped, and with bundles of troubles in his trembling, withered hands.

Perhaps, on his halting, tenuous way, the old man may lose from one of his bundles a bitterly cold morning here; a light smattering of snow there; or an immensely cold and blustery day, a day when the towering waves of Lake Superior stand many feet high before crashing down on land, depositing the flotsam and jetsam of months of quiet summer waves far above the high water line of eroded and deserted beaches.

The old man retrieves his early, wayward troubles, for their time has not yet come. The scene returns to the soft and gentle autumn sunlight and the quiet days once more, lulling the foolish people into believing that this was temporary, only a momentary aberration.

Slowly the truth begins to dawn on the foolish people, as their cars refuse to start and as their furnaces kick on. But summer can't be gone so soon, they cry, in their surprise and their anxiety.

Why, the people protest, it was autumn only yesterday! The hardwoods were clothed in vibrant colors; the apples were hanging heavily from the branches; the grouse were rocketing from thickets in front of eager dogs; and the buck deer were pursuing the does excitedly, with their necks swollen and their antlers gleaming in the sun. No, no, they exclaim, there must be some mistake! There is too much left to do, we are not ready!

But old man winter is not dissuaded. He slowly unpacks his bundles of woes with his trembling hands and moves into the bare and abandoned house of autumn.

The old man covers the ripened fruit, the fat grouse, the backs of the deer, and the tired leaves lying deep beneath the stark hardwoods with the frost from his beard, and he freezes the watercourses with his cold and aged breath. He sets out his meager possessions: the depression that he takes with him everywhere, and the time that runs ever so slowly; as the sunlight extinguishes, and the water pipes freeze, and the gas and the electric meters whirl.

It is quiet in the house of autumn now. The old man sits in silence on a bare wooden chair on his bony and emaciated flanks, with his head bowed and silver and with his body chilling as his last reserves of warmth extinguish; reminiscing of better times, and waiting for merciful death to come.

*   *   *   *

Beneath the glass-like surface of the frozen lake, the huge fish swam slowly, unconcerned and unhurried. *Nah Ma*, a giant lake sturgeon, was the lord of Lake Gogebic, and all other creatures gave way before his majestic presence. Purposefully, he made its way towards the two small circles of light in the obsidian roof above him, his curiosity piqued.

At over eight feet long and weighing in excess of three hundred pounds, the great fish was superbly adapted to his environment. He was the product of a genetic chain that had stretched unbroken from the Jurassic era for a hundred million years. One hundred and forty years old, he was ancient, even by long-lived sturgeon standards.

Nah Ma was the chance survivor of a pairing of sturgeons who had fled upstream, through the passage permitted in an Ojibwa fishing weir located some four miles from the mouth of the Ontonagon River at Lake Superior, many generations before. It was long before the West Branch, the outlet of Lake Gogebic, and the South Branch of that river that it converged with, had been dammed, both for power and to maintain the level of the largest lake in the Upper Peninsula.

The Ojibwa fishing weir had been made of tightly intertwined saplings and small trees, pounded into the clay bottom of the stream. It had been constructed in a manner that allowed the sturgeon to move upstream through it during their yearly spring spawning run, but then to intercept the fish and prevent their uninterrupted return to the big lake on their way downstream.

The Ojibwa fishermen would maneuver on top of the weir. They would wait to feel the vibrations of the big fish, as they impacted both the weir and the long wooden poles, with hooks at the ends, that they held in their hands. Large numbers of sturgeon would be snagged in this way every spring following their spawning rituals, rituals that did not occur until the adult fish were already about twenty-five years old.

The Ojibwa were a forest tribe that depended on the sturgeon for a variety of food and materials, in the same way that that the prairie tribes depended on the buffalo. The Ojibwa revered the sturgeon and called it *Nah Ma*, the King of Fishes. From it they obtained meat, skin for leather, oil, and waterproofing, the latter of which was derived from a fluid in its bladder.

The arrival of the white man in the Ontonagon country had changed everything, for both the Ojibwa and for the lake sturgeon. The rivers were dammed, and the fish's migration routes were blocked.

Commercial fishermen of Lake Superior reviled the lake sturgeon for blundering into their nets, destroying them in the process. Entangled sturgeon were slaughtered and left to rot, so many that ships sometimes had to be used to haul the decomposing corpses to other waters to allow continued fishing. Sturgeon were piled on the beaches, doused with kerosene and then set aflame, and steamships had them stacked like cordwood on deck to fire their boilers.

Belatedly, the white man discovered that the roe of the lake sturgeon was similar to that of the Russian beluga sturgeon and could be made into equally prized caviar, and that its meat tasted like the finest veal. The skins, they learned, could be tanned into fine-grade leather, to be made into handbags, shoes and belts then sold on the East Coast and in Europe. Isinglass, the gelatinous substance found in the bladder of the lake sturgeon, became used to clarify beer and wine, to cement pottery, and to set jellies. It also became important in the manufacture of carriage and early automobile windows.

But by this time it was too late for the lake sturgeon, just as it was too late for the Ojibwa. The great fish is now rare wherever it is found. States now struggle to reintroduce them to waters where they once ranged freely, in uncountable numbers.

Nah Ma, the giant sturgeon, was the only one of his kind in the entire thirteen thousand acres of mighty Lake Gogebic, the *Agogebik* of the Ojibwa, in the former lands of Hiawatha. Lake Gogebic had been a haven for the mighty fish for all of his one hundred forty years. Its dark waters concealed him from both man and other predators. The deep, former river channel on the east side of the lake sheltered him from summer heat. The vast mud flats of mid-lake abounded with billions of mayfly larvae, bloodworms, crustaceans, mollusks, snails and small fish, a smorgasbord of sturgeon favorites that had allowed him to reach the maximum size possible for his species.

The fishermen of Lake Gogebic posed no threat to *Nah Ma* in their pursuit of the walleye, pike, smallmouth bass and perch that thrive in the lake. The great fish was so large that the fisherman simply could not recognize him as a living thing on their fish finders and other electronic devices. *Nah Ma*, the giant lake sturgeon, was completely out of proportion to anything else that could reasonably be expected to live in the big lake. Unthreatened by man, or by the rigors and hazards of the spawning season, the fish had become inordinately huge, the gentle ruler of his watery kingdom.

As the great fish approached the twin circles of light in the roof of his world, he absently noted the two small sucker minnows swimming feebly beneath the lights, about a foot from the muddy bottom. Since the small fish were too high for easy intake into his enormous, underslung, vacuum cleaner-like mouth, he simply chose to ignore them. Food was never a high priority to *Nah Ma* in his rich domain.

Slowly and ponderously, *Nah Ma* came to a halt beneath the light circles, motionless, like a vast, inert submarine. The almost invisible monofilament leader that suspended one of the sucker minnows beneath its hole in the ice then played along one side of the five rows of overlapping plates, the scutes, that ran along the entire length of his body.

In the small portable ice fishing shanty above the two holes cut in the ice, Sidney Hornberg sat on an overturned bucket in the glare of a propane lantern, oblivious to the presence of the great fish beneath him. Hornberg stared forlornly at the two yellow slip bobbers as they made their way in slow wobbles around the holes, propelled by the small sucker minnows suspended below. They looked, Hornberg thought with distaste, like egg yolks skidding around two small, black frying pans. My God, he asked himself for the hundredth time, why did I ever agree to this insanity?

Outside, somewhere in the blackness of the night, he could hear Paul Adams cackling, quietly and happily, as he wrestled with some unseen fish at the end of his tipup line. Adams seemed to be in his natural element, Hornberg thought; on a night so black that a man couldn't see one foot, a frozen night lit only by starlight in the middle of an equally frozen lake, a winter scene that seemed to him to be as desolate as a moonscape.

This is no place for a city boy, Hornberg thought miserably. His back was beginning to ache from his unnatural position on top of the overturned bucket. This is about as exciting as watching paint dry, Hornberg pouted. He briefly reviewed how it had come to pass that he now found his posterior parked on a bucket, in the middle of this huge, godforsaken lake, as the bobbers continued their slow, wobbly orbits around the holes in the ice.

Earlier that day, Paul Adams, the Michigan State Police detective, had been overtly casual but strangely insistent at the same time. Hornberg needed to get out of the office, he had said. He needed to get out of Marquette, to get away from this 'Gregor' thing for an evening. He needed to get out into the great frosty outdoors of the Upper Peninsula, to savor the winter in the manner that the locals did, in order to "break him out of his paradigm". Since this was completely out of character for his friend and colleague, having known and worked with the man for several years, a small voice in the back of Hornberg's mind had finally convinced him, reluctantly, to go along with Adams' proposed ice fishing jaunt on this night to Lake Gogebic.

They had met at the car pool parking lot south of L'Anse at the State Highway M-28 junction, about two hours before sunset. After greeting Hornberg, Adams had opened the back door of the topper behind his pickup truck's cab and had thrown in Hornberg's winter clothes, boots, and his small cooler containing his carefully packed lunch that had been packed with affection by his wife. "Be careful out there with that jack pine savage, Paul Adams," she had admonished him with fake concern.

Glancing into the pickup topper, Hornberg had seen an incredible tangle of ice fishing poles, tipups, skis, buckets, augers, propane bottles, lanterns, heaters, and various boxes and bags of non-descript parts and fabrics that offered no readily discernable function to Hornberg. My God, the man is moving out of his house, Hornberg had thought, despairingly. How long is he planning on keeping me out there?

The trip west had been taken up by small talk, with each man carefully avoiding any mention of 'Gregor' or the Ukrainian physicist that the mystery man sought, somewhere in the Upper Peninsula. "I usually fish Portage Lake, since it's right by Houghton," Adams had said casually, "but the ice isn't very good there yet. Gogebic is a bit of a hike for us, but the fishing is usually pretty good, and the ice sets up way before Portage does."

Adams had then expounded at length on the thrilling nature of the ice fishing experience in general, including a detailed explanation of the piscatorial mysteries involved in catching the wily walleye. Adams had waxed poetic about the exquisite flavor of their firm white flesh, including several of his favorite ways to prepare this apparently magical fish. Hornberg had assumed that this was Adams' way of taking his mind off of the case, and he had gladly gone along with it, enjoying the light banter.

Hornberg had good reason to not want to think about the 'Gregor' fiasco for a while. The man called Gregor and his cohorts had gone to ground, as if they had somehow vanished from the face of the earth.

No further calls to Hornberg had occurred. Over two thousand called-up National Guard troops and state and local police had carefully combed every known hunting and fishing camp, rental property, hotel, motel, and campsite in the entire Upper Peninsula and in northern Wisconsin for weeks, at great expense, with no result.

Hornberg and the other officials now generally assumed that the mystery group had quietly been assimilated into one of the many Russian and Ukrainian communities on both sides of the U.S.-Canadian border, communities known to be tight-lipped to outsiders, to await the next phase of whatever they had planned. What that next phase might consist of, American law enforcement had no clue.

The CIA man, Wilton, and Army Colonel Wenzel had continued to be frustratingly secretive about the facts concerning the Ukrainian physicist, Doctor Sergei Lysenko, or his present whereabouts. Many heated discussions between Hornberg, Adams, and the "two spooks," as Adams had taken to irreverently calling them, had occurred over giving them the information they had requested.

"Goddammit!" Adams had exploded, at one meeting. "How do you assholes expect us to help you if we don't know who or what it is we're trying to protect?" Each such meeting, however, had ended on the same acrimonious note: a curt reply from the CIA man that they had "no need to know." Hornberg and Adams would leave each such encounter fuming and resentful.

The trip west to the big lake had passed uneventfully. After leaving Kenton, Bruce Crossing, and Ewen in their wakes, the two men had pulled into the small community of Bergland that sits at the head of twenty-mile-long Lake Gogebic.

The two men had made a quick stop at the only bait shop on the entire lake in order to buy a fishing license for Hornberg and to purchase the small sucker minnows that were the favorite food of Gogebic's winter walleyes, according to Adams. They then headed down State Highway M-64, running north and south along the west side of the big lake, to Adams' "secret spot."

After getting into his winter clothes, Hornberg had watched in amazement as Adams deposited the entire contents of the pickup topper on the snow-covered ground beside the truck. The two men then moved the entire assemblage, as many pieces at a time as each could carry, the several hundred yards to the shore of the frozen lake, and then another four hundred yards offshore to the area that they would fish that evening. Several trips had been necessary to move all of the gear. Hornberg was sweating beneath his winter clothes by the time all the moves had been completed, despite the temperature that hovered around zero degrees. At least there's no wind, Hornberg had thought, gratefully.

After setting up a small portable fishing shanty, Adams had fired up his gasoline-powered ice auger. He had then drilled a preposterous number of eight inch diameter holes through the twelve inch thick ice all over the immediate area, including two spaced closely together that he slid the shanty over. Hornberg was baffled; the regulations that he had just read clearly stated that only two fishing lines per person were permitted. "Never know which ones are going to be the hot holes, Sid," Adams had explained, seriously, as Hornberg watched the operation and began to doubt his friend's sanity. The sun was now well set, and it was growing blacker by the minute.

After cleaning out the ice holes in the shanty, Adams had lit a small propane heater and set it in one corner, well away from the plastic fabric of the shanty walls. He then lit a propane lantern, hanging it from the center brace of the shanty with an s-hook. He procured two buckets for seating from somewhere in the massive pile of gear on the ice and then sat down in the shanty with Hornberg, the minnow bucket, and two short spinning rods equipped with slip bobbers, lead shot, and small treble hooks at the end of short monofilament leaders. This is like playing handball in a shower with two players, Hornberg thought with some amusement, as he sat cramped next to Adams on his bucket seat.

After setting the depth of the slip bobbers, Adams had carefully skewered a sucker minnow on the treble hook of each line. He then had gently lowered each minnow down into the inky black water of the lake, until the slip bobber suspended it about a foot from the lake bottom.

As the slip bobbers began to wobble about in the ice holes, with each doomed sucker minnow frantically trying to reach the safety of the lake bottom, Adams had then wedged the rod handles above them between the center brace and the roof fabric of the shanty. He opened the reel bails so that the line would play out freely if a fish took the bait.

When Adams opened the zippered entrance door to attend to his tipups in the outside blackness, Hornberg had just been able to make out through the gloaming that the few other fishermen that had been fishing in the area when they had arrived were now making their way off of the lake. They were dragging their equipment on skids behind them as they walked, or drove their ATVs on the icy surface.

"Yeah, well," Adams had explained, with apparent conviction, in response to Hornberg's question, "those guys are leaving way too early, the real bite doesn't start until after eight p.m. They've probably got to work tomorrow." Yeah, right, Hornberg had thought, somewhat viciously; or maybe they're just not completely nuts, like we are.

Adams had then left through the entrance door and had disappeared into the black night to set his two tipups, away from the shanty but close enough to be illuminated by a flashlight. Hornberg was left alone inside, with his thoughts and the two short rods, as the bobbers wobbled around in the holes in the ice.

The interior of the shanty was warming quickly now, from the heat of both the lantern and the small heater. Hornberg found himself suddenly shedding his outside clothes, perspiring in the sudden heat, until it occurred to him to use the entrance door zippers at each end of the shanty to regulate the temperature inside.

Now, some thirty minutes later, Hornberg had to admit that it was actually quite comfortable inside the shanty, except for his aching back. He was dreading the trip off the ice later with all of their gear, when the night would be even colder and darker.

It was a little boring out here, perhaps, Hornberg thought absently, but it was definitely comfortable. In an odd way, he could somewhat understand why his friend, Paul Adams, valued ice fishing so highly. If a man craved occasional solitude, this was definitely it.

Hornberg's lunch, which he had eaten inside the close confines while watching the bobbers go round and round, had been excellent as usual, for his wife was a fine cook. From experimenting with the little heater, the lantern, and the zippered entrance doors, he had finally gotten the temperature control figured out. It was quite mesmerizing, and almost hypnotic, Hornberg thought, to watch the bobbers as they made their separate ways around the holes. With his belly full and his long day behind him, he sleepily pictured what the scene might be like at the bottom of the dark lake.

Hornberg's mind was freewheeling and almost completely blank, as if it were resting and erasing the memory of recent events. If I nod off, I'll probably fall face down in one of these stupid holes and drown, he thought, with wry amusement. There might actually be some value in this kind of 'therapy' after all, he concluded, grudgingly.

Paul Adams was obviously enjoying himself immensely. Already, one small walleye, a barely legal 'eater', according to Adams, was slowly stiffening on the ice beside the shanty's entrance door in the frigid night air. It had been taken on one of the outside tipups, while Adams had held a flashlight in his mouth to work with the line in the dark.

A walleye is an interesting-looking fish, Hornberg told himself, as he looked at the small fish through a crack in the zippered entrance. Its flanks were colored burnished antique gold, and it had gleaming white stripes on the anal fin and the tip of the tail. The mirrored eyes that give the fish its name, from a reflective membrane behind the retina, the *tapetum lucidum*, that gathers and reflects light, gleamed brightly in the light of the lantern.

Its mouth open from one last, frozen gasp, the small walleye displayed its fearsome, conical teeth. I'll bet that one of these guys can catch just about anything that it wants to, Hornberg thought, with amused and idle admiration; too bad we can't latch one on Gregor's sick ass!

As Hornberg continued his quiet musings, the bobber directly in front of him suddenly stopped its now barely discernable movements in the ice hole and slowly submerged, as if taken down by some great weight. Hornberg quickly mentally reviewed Adams' careful instructions that he had given during the car trip to Bergland.

"A walleye will grab the sucker and run off with it a little way, and then he'll stop and kill it," Adams had told him. "Then he'll turn it and get it going down his throat head first and move off a little further. When he's got it well down he'll take off, looking for his next meal. When he starts moving that third time, close the reel bail, take up the slack line until you feel him, and then set the hook!" he had concluded fiercely, with an animated hand gesture to make his point.

Hornberg watched carefully as the bobber disappeared beneath the ice, waiting for the first pause of the fish. But the pause did not come. As the minutes passed by, yard after yard of line slowly and constantly peeled from the spinning reel that he now held in his hand, and still there was no pause. There's got to be a hundred feet of line out by this time, Hornberg thought, in confusion; better to wait and get Paul's opinion when he comes back.

After a short time, Hornberg heard the crunching sound of Adam's boots on the snow-covered lake as he made his way back to the shanty. Then he heard a dull thud, followed by flopping sounds, as a second walleye joined its now-frozen brother on the ice.

"This one's a good one, probably twenty inches or so," Adams said to Hornberg, happily, through the zippered entrance door. "Man, Sid, you're going to be a real hero when you take these tasty devils home. Emma might even give you some," Adams commented, with an evil chuckle, his double entendre completely intended. "How are you doing in there?" he asked, from the darkness.

"I miss my wife, I miss my bed, and I miss my wife in my bed," Hornberg lamented forlornly.

Adams laughed and then shouted "Whiner!" from the blackness outside the shanty. "How's everything else going? Any bites?"

"I think I've got something going on right now, you had better take a look," Hornberg replied, as he watched the line continued its steady progress away beneath the ice.

A sudden blast of cold air jolted Hornberg as the door zipper was ripped open. Adams stuck his bare head through the entrance, supporting himself from the shanty frame with his bare arms, his shirtsleeves rolled back. Adams' cheeks were ruddy from the cold, and he looked like some kind of wild Viking, with his blond hair in disarray and a large smile on his face, completely in his element on the frozen lake. He was obviously comfortable in only a shirt in the frigid night air, Hornberg saw, air that was cold enough to freeze a living fish solid within minutes.

Adams observed the scene inside for a few seconds, and then he asked, quietly, as if the fish could hear him, "How many times has he stopped?"

"He hasn't," Hornberg replied in confusion, as the line continued to disappear beneath the ice.

"How long has he been on?" asked Adams, his fisherman's natural curiosity now thoroughly aroused.

"More than ten minutes," responded Hornberg, as he glanced quickly at his watch.

"Holy wah, Sid, that fish has got the sucker down to his butthole by this time!" Adams exclaimed, now in a loud voice. "OK, like we talked about, close the bail, take up the slack, and zuff him!" he continued excitedly.

As instructed, Hornberg closed the reel bail and took in the slack line until he felt the fish at the other end of the line. Then he set the hook firmly and deliberately, but a heavy weight was all that he felt.

The short rod slowly bent straight down into the ice hole, as the two men looked on in amazement. Then the reel's drag began to sing, ever so slowly, at a steady rate, as the line continued to disappear beneath the ice.

"My Christ, Sid, what have you got on there, the SS Silversides?" asked Adams, awe in his voice. "That's no walleye. By God, it's got to be Jaws!" he exclaimed excitedly.

Adams was referring to a legendary Gogebic pike that he had told Hornberg about during the car trip. It supposedly inhabited the weeds of Bergland Bay at the north end of the lake, a pike big enough to tow boats. It purportedly showed itself several times each summer, to terrorize fishermen and to relieve them of their expensive fishing tackle. Adams had always believed that the pike was a convenient rumor, invented by Bergland businesses to keep the tourists interested. But, as he watched Hornberg struggle with this fish, he was no longer so certain.

"Paul, I can't do anything with this beast!" exclaimed Hornberg in desperation. The short rod was bent so acutely beginning at the reel seat that it must surely break, and his wrists ached from the effort of not letting go of the rod.

"Well, there's nothing else for it but to tighten down the drag," Adams advised him. "You've got to try to turn him, you're almost out of line," he added ominously, noting that the shiny metal of the reel spool had only several turns of line left around it.

As he had been instructed, Hornberg tightened the drag on the reel. Adams now watched in amazement as Hornberg was slowly dragged towards the hole in the ice. When all of the stretch had been removed from the long line it suddenly went limp, and the fish was gone.

Below their feet, the giant lake sturgeon, *Nah Ma*, slowly and calmly continued on his night's journey. The great fish was completely unaware that a veteran agent of the Federal Bureau of Investigation had briefly attempted to apprehend him, for he could not feel the tiny treble hook beneath the scute on his side. Human concerns were irrelevant to the King of Fishes, in any case.

After Hornberg had reeled in the two hundred feet of line that the giant fish had pulled off the reel, the men saw that the monofilament leader had broken cleanly at the lead shot. Both men sat on their buckets in the portable shanty, completely spent.

"Well, Sid, I think we might as well pack it in for the night," Adams said, tiredly. "I don't think that we're going to be able to top that fish."

Hornberg wordlessly agreed, nodding his head as he massaged his aching wrists. Both men then sat quietly on their overturned buckets for several minutes, reflecting, until Hornberg finally broke the silence. "Okay, Paul, why did you really drag me out here tonight?" he asked the policeman, quizzically, as he looked directly at his friend.

Adams returned his gaze. After a long moment, Adams answered. "Is your cell phone on, Sid?" he asked the FBI man, mysteriously.

"Of course," replied Hornberg, patting the shirt pocket on his chest where the small phone resided, to stay warm. Both men never went anywhere without their cell phones, for they were as indispensable to them in their official capacity as any other tool of their trade. And, unlike most civilian cell phones in the Upper Peninsula, their phones could reach them anywhere, anytime.

"Good. Then they know exactly where we are, two nut cases sitting in the middle of a frozen lake in the middle of the night. Just what I want them to think," Adams stated flatly, satisfaction in his voice.

"Who is this 'they' that you're talking about, Paul?" Hornberg asked, puzzled.

"I'll get to that in a second," Adams responded, mysteriously. "Sid," he continued quietly, "your car is bugged, both voice and location. So is mine."

Hornberg accepted the information without surprise. Although he hadn't specifically been informed, it was to be expected that 'the spooks', as Adams referred to them, would keep tabs on them, in case 'Gregor' decided to pay another visit. "So?" he asked, without emotion.

"It's worse than that," Adams elaborated, in a quiet tone, his voice expressionless. "Your house is bugged, too. Bedroom, living room, and that chair on the front porch that you like to sit in; visual, audio, the whole ball of wax. Your phone is tapped, also. Our lab guys found the stuff," Adams continued, unhappily.

Hornberg felt the heat rising into his face, as his pulse quickened and the pounding began in his ears. A deep sense of outrage slowly filled his entire consciousness. "You went through my house, Paul?" Hornberg asked, quietly and ominously, as he stared at the man. He felt betrayed. "You didn't happen to have a search warrant, did you?"

"Ah, actually no, Sid," Adams responded, guiltily. "They would have known if I had asked for one."

A long silence now fell on the close confines of the small shelter, as Hornberg processed this information. The pounding in his ears reached a crescendo. He thought, with deep moral outrage, of his middle-aged, fumbling attempts at lovemaking with his wife and the occasional recriminations common in any marriage, recorded for the amusement of some unseen observer.

"Why, Paul?" hissed Hornberg, furious.

"I played a hunch," replied Adams, softly, shrugging his shoulders. "We are both being controlled, like we're bait," he continued morosely, motioning with a hand to the one remaining yellow slip bobber wobbling about its ice hole.

Slowly Hornberg regained a measure of control as he struggled to suppress the instinct to strike out at his friend, who sat quietly beside him on his overturned bucket, looking sheepish, as if expecting Hornberg to do exactly that. From some distant place within his mind he heard himself say, quietly and rationally, carefully framing each word: "You were lucky Emma didn't catch you in our house, Paul. She doesn't deserve to be dragged into this. Who did this to us? Gregor?" he demanded of his friend, fiercely.

"We don't think so," replied Adams, softly. "The stuff we found in your house and car is all American-made. I'm guessing that it's our spook friends," he concluded, miserably.

Briefly the sense of outrage washed over Hornberg again, before his police instincts took over and forced him to look at the situation objectively. It just made no sense. "Why would they do that, Paul?" he asked, in confusion.

"Sid," his friend responded, gently, "I may be just a small town cop, but I didn't just fall off the turnip wagon. Wilton and Wenzel don't want us anywhere near their Ukrainian, that's pretty clear, right?"

"Right," replied Hornberg, struggling to see where Adams was going with his train of thought. The CIA man and the Army colonel had made it obvious to both of them that they had no need to know anything about the foreign scientist.

"Well, I think that they've got plans for this guy, and they're not good plans," Adams continued, crossing his arms as if to make his point. "Once this poor bastard has served his purpose, whatever that is, he's history," he concluded, grimly.

Hornberg considered this carefully. It might just fit, he thought. With his many years of Federal service, Hornberg was no stranger to the occasional 'wet work' that his government found to be necessary in its dealings with other international players.

"And Gregor? What is his part in this?" Hornberg asked, his mind racing ahead.

"Think about it, Sid!" Adams continued, emphatically. "Why did these assholes bring nukes into the country with them? They're not here to take this Ukrainian back with them, they're here to kill him!"

"And they don't know exactly where he is, or under what circumstances he's being kept in," Hornberg added, making the logical leap. "So, by using a small tactical nuke, all they have to do is get close!" he concluded, revelation finally parting his confusion, like the morning sun melting away the fog.

"Bingo!" exclaimed Adams, animatedly. "Four-Oh! This poor bastard is a dead man, either way. Either our guys 'off' him or they do, along with everybody else in the blast radius!"

The two men sat in silence for a few moments, side by side on their overturned buckets. "This guy must be awfully important," said Hornberg finally, as Adams nodded in agreement. "Tell, me, Paul, do you have any more surprises for me tonight?"

"Yeah, Sid, just one more," Adams replied, as if in afterthought. "I think I know where they're keeping him."

Hornberg blinked, startled. "You do?" he asked in surprise. "Where?"

"Not many miles from here, actually," Adams replied, matter-of-factly. "It's in a chunk of woods in the Sylvania Wilderness, over by Watersmeet. There's some sort of research station back in there off a county road; supposedly, a couple of universities are studying trees."

"Some locals called our Wakefield Post," Adams explained, "and said that they thought some kind of drug activity was going on in the area; strange cars around at odd hours, etcetera. We checked it out and, what do you know, they're Feds!" Adams continued, with a small smile. "It looks like they've got some kind of loose surveillance going on around the whole area. No good reason for it that we know of, and, of course, the spooks aren't talking."

"Paul, you never cease to amaze me," Hornberg replied, in genuine admiration. "You're way ahead of me on this one. What now?" he asked his friend.

"Now, you and I go in there tomorrow and scope it out for ourselves," Adams replied, his eyes locked with Hornberg's.

"So we just barge in and say, hey, we hear that you've got some poor Ukrainian scientist, who is soon to be very dead, locked up back here?" asked Hornberg, sarcastically.

"No," replied Adams, calmly. "We go in quietly. In camouflage. Sneaky-peeky. If this poor Ukrainian bastard has a chance in hell, it's going to have to be us, I think," he concluded, grimly.

Hornberg's head swam. The nightmare continues, he thought hopelessly. "What's your plan?" he asked Adams.

"There's a bar that I frequent occasionally in Kenton called Jumpy's, right on the way back," explained Adams, in response. "We'll stop there for a couple of hours. The spooks will know that we're there, of course. Tomorrow, we'll both call in sick first thing in the morning and claim that we were over-served and have hangovers."

"You're not helping my next performance appraisal, Paul," said Hornberg, wryly.

"You're fifty-four and a half, Sid, you don't have a next performance appraisal," replied Adams, with a grin. "I'll borrow an unmarked car from the motor pool tonight and meet you down the block from your house in front of the deli at 0800. Leave your cell phone home tomorrow, we don't want them to know that we're coming."

*   *   *   *

The televisions behind the bar droned on in a dull crescendo of background noise, a NASCAR rerun on one set and an inane network show on the other. No one was watching either set.

Except for the two men, the bar was empty. The slender young woman would have closed up, if she could only get these fellows to take a hint; however, they did not appear to be in any hurry to leave. She busied herself behind the bar, cleaning up and organizing.

She slightly knew the one man, Paul Adams, who sat at a table filleting two mostly frozen and not overly large walleyes on newspaper while working on his fourth beer. Adams came in occasionally. Although he had never said so straight out, she could tell that he was a cop. In her business, she had of necessity become a good judge of character.

Adams was a big, blond, and very good looking man, she thought, a bit admiringly, always with a smile on his face and a little swagger in his walk. But, there was something about the way that he took over the room with his presence, and the way that some of the local patrons looked around furtively for an escape route when he came in, that gave him away.

Still, Jumpy's Bar in Kenton was neutral ground for police and perpetrators alike. Things had to degenerate considerably before she would even consider calling 911. Although she weighed only eighty pounds soaking wet, Angie the bartender had both the heart of a lion and a sixteen-inch section of heavy hardwood chair rail within ready reach behind the bar.

The other man was new to her. Sid, he'd told her, before lapsing into silence, nursing a scotch and rubbing his forehead while gazing bemusedly at the graffiti on the ceiling tiles above his head. No big tips tonight, Angie knew.

This man was a puzzle, she thought to herself. It was hard to see him running with the big, blond, Nordic god who was cleaning the fish at the table across from the bar, chattering incessantly about the latest activities of his wife and kids to no one in particular.

Not overly large, the balding man who had called himself Sid seemed to be shrinking before her eyes as he gazed at the ceiling tiles, covered wall-to-wall with graffiti, above him. They were the work of hundreds of camp drunks over many years, each with their own ceiling tile, she had told him. They had been a casual joke that had exploded as each camp tried to outdo the others, and they had made Jumpy's the destination bar of both locals and visitors alike to this part of the western Upper Peninsula.

She had watched as 'Sid' stared at the last ceiling tile above the back door of the place. It was a piercing stare, almost as if to ignite it, as though he recognized the piece, a tile signed by an 'A. Tinanen'. The panel was dark and brooding; a glimpse into a deranged mind, with blood and body parts everywhere. It was completely out of place among the many others, all of which were dedicated lightly, and in some cases obscenely, to hunting, fishing, drinking, and fornicating in this last great Midwest forest refuge; expressions of their creators' collective illusion of what the Upper Peninsula still was, in these modern times.

This 'Sid' guy is a heart attack looking for a place to happen, Angie thought to herself, as she watched him fixate on the tile by the back door. She turned off the televisions and extinguished the light behind the bar; maybe these two would finally get the message.

*   *   *   *

In the darkness of the well-appointed apartment in the Landmark Inn in Marquette, lit only by a small gas fireplace in the corner, the phone jangled on the nightstand. Bruce Wilton of the Central Intelligence Agency was instantly awake and alert, his almost Pavlovian response honed by years of secret service to his country.

Glancing at the numbers on the phone's liquid crystal display, Wilton quickly checked them against a small book tabbed with the day's date. Once he had authenticated the call, he pushed the 'talk' button and answered, "Wilton."

"Thor," the disembodied voice answered, mechanically. "The people in Seattle have everything they need. 'The Package' is now a liability. Have the Indian eliminate him." The phone clicked, and a dull drone rang in Wilton's ear.

Wilton hung up the phone and rubbed his eyes. Time to call Wenzel down the hall from him and then grab a quick shower, for it would be a long day; he had been expecting this call for some time. They would need to drive all the way to Watersmeet on this day and give the Indian his instructions.

CHAPTER 11

▼

"Motheeer!" the young girl's high-pitched voice shrieked. It wailed down the stairs and into the kitchen like a fire siren, assaulting the woman's ears as she stood at the counter making sandwiches for their lunches in the early morning blackness. "Jenna won't let me in the bathroom!" the young voice protested loudly. "She's been in there for hours!"

"Oh, grow up, Kati!" said Jenna, the offender, haughtily, through the locked bathroom door, to her younger sister. "You know perfectly well that I'm getting my class pictures taken today!"

"Just stop it, the both of you!" said their mother, without looking up from her task. The remonstration was almost automatic, a normal part of the morning ritual known as getting her daughters off to school and herself to work. The squabble over teenager turf was as much an inevitable part of daily life in their home as were the sack lunches that she was making. "You'll wake your father, and he didn't get much sleep last night!" Not likely, she thought to herself privately, chuckling under her breath; a cannon next to his ear couldn't wake that man up right now.

Elizabeth Bergstrom-Adams had just finished bagging the three lunches when her seventeen-year-old daughter, Jenna, flounced down the stairs in her class picture finery. The bathroom door slammed behind her as her younger daughter, Kati, claimed that prized territory.

Elizabeth looked her oldest daughter over carefully, as the young woman glided into the kitchen like the Queen of the Nile. She clucked her tongue in mock reproach; too much makeup, too much jewelry, and those pants couldn't be any tighter if they had been spray-painted on, she thought, despondently. She glanced despairingly at the little bit of belly that showed above the top of her daughter's slacks. Why did girls nowadays think that dressing like streetwalkers made them attractive, she thought hopelessly?

For all of that, though, Jenna was a beautiful young woman, her mother had to admit. At over six feet, Jenna stood a full foot and a half taller than her tiny mother, with long legs and a striking figure. Her long, brunette hair and dark eyes were in striking contrast to both of her parents' Slavic, light blond features, a fact that generated the usual amount of hospital crib-switching ribbing for their family. But she definitely got her height from her father, Paul, the big, blond, Michigan State Police detective, Elizabeth knew.

A good student and a top athlete, Jenna was virtually assured of a basketball scholarship to hometown Michigan Technological University upon her high school graduation this year. This fact both greatly pleased her parents and slightly dismayed Jenna, to whom Houghton, Michigan was beginning to look a little too small and too close to home, now that she had her drivers license and her little hatchback car.

"Now, don't forget that you've got to pick Kati up from band practice after school," Elizabeth addressed her oldest daughter, handing her a lunch bag, as eleven-year-old Kati came bouncing down the stairs carrying a clarinet case. Kati was a tiny replica of Elizabeth herself, with short, blond hair and blue eyes. She was a tightly wound bundle of nervous energy, with scabs on her knees and with her thin, childish figure still undeveloped. Kati was an indifferent student, and she still thought that boys were "gross!" The two girls could not have been more dissimilar, their parents were well aware.

"Yes, mother, I'll pick the little twerp up," said Jenna, derisively, as Elizabeth handed a lunch bag to Kati, just as the young girl was sticking her tongue out at Jenna. "You know, Kati," Jenna added in a superior tone, with an arched eyebrow, "if you keep sticking that thing out at me, it's going to freeze in this cold weather, and a pigeon is going to crap on it!"

"Jenna!" said her mother, reproachfully, as the defiant Kati stuck her tongue out once more at her older sister. "You're just as much at fault as she is. Now off you go. Drive carefully, it's icy out there this morning."

"Yes, mother," the girls echoed each other, as they kissed Elizabeth on each cheek and headed for the front door. "Don't you make me late tonight, you little twerp, I've got a basketball game!" Jenna warned her sister, punching a knuckle into the young girl's shoulder as the door opened.

"Ow! *Motheeer!*" was the last clear sound that Elizabeth heard as the front door clicked shut. My God, what a dysfunctional family, she thought to herself, shaking her head in mock dismay. Jenna's little car started up in the driveway, finally drowning out the sibling dispute, and it then slowly backed out.

Alone now in the quiet of the kitchen, Elizabeth tidied up the countertop and put the few dishes in the sink, as the two family cats finally came out of hiding, no longer afraid of being trampled in the morning stampede. Her mind unconsciously played back the last familiar 'dysfunctional family' theme while she opened a can of Friskies and bent to feed the cats on the floor.

It had always been that way for them, she reflected, as the cats attacked the food. No one in her hometown of Ontonagon would have ever put tiny, serious, goal-oriented Elizabeth Bergstrom together with big, blond, and boisterous Paul Adams.

At the time, Paul had been back from the Marine Corps for almost two years and was a recent graduate of the Michigan State Police Academy. Paul had always been the Houghton hometown hero and jock extraordinaire: flamboyant, extraverted, and adored by all of the girls in the surrounding four counties. Conversely, most of Elizabeth's casual friends had concluded by the end of high school that she was inevitably destined to die alone, a virginal librarian.

Fate takes some funny twists and turns, Elizabeth had always thought. She had not had a particularly happy girlhood in Ontonagon. Her fisherman father, Marcus Bergstrom, had disappeared there on Lake Superior during a storm long ago, leaving her mother a young widow and herself and her two sisters fatherless.

The Bergstrom uncles and family friends had done what they could, and the town and its many churches were very supportive. But the other village residents had their own to worry about, and so things had been difficult for them. Not impossible, of course, for the village of Ontonagon looked after its own, but still difficult. Even to this day, Elizabeth could hardly bear to throw anything away. She still patched worn clothing and let things out, as she had learned from her mother at a very young age.

On dark mornings in a warm kitchen, such as today, it was almost as if Elizabeth still smelled her father's distinctive and peculiar diesel odor, an odor that was an unavoidable consequence of his daily fishing aboard the oil-fired, family fish tug *Anna M.*, wafting down the stairs as he headed out for the Bergstrom family dock on the Ontonagon River. That unmistakable odor was one of her strongest memories of the man; she had smelled it almost every day until she was five years old. Then, suddenly, everything had changed for her, one stormy late June day in Ontonagon.

And then, long after her father's disappearance and over ten years after graduating from high school, everything had changed for Elizabeth again. One day, Elizabeth Bergstrom, twenty-eight years old and still unmarried, was working at the front desk of the Ontonagon County Courthouse, as she had every day for the previous nine years, when twenty-four year old Paul Adams, a Michigan State Police rookie, came through the front door to prosecute a minor traffic charge.

Elizabeth remembered that day as if it were yesterday, she recalled fondly. The dull, official room had taken on a glow when the big, blond policeman strode in as if he were king of all he surveyed, resplendent in his taut blue uniform. He had glanced at her and then had simply stood there, transfixed. And that was all it had taken.

Elizabeth still had a hard time believing that it had all happened, so long ago. They had been so very different. While she had been almost painfully shy, Paul was outgoing and boisterous, and he was on a first name basis with county deputies and judges alike after a single conversation.

Before meeting Paul, Elizabeth had always hated the outdoors. She remembered the harsh Ontonagon winters and the mostly bare cupboards in the tiny, and occasionally chilly, Ontonagon house that her mother, her sisters, and she had shared. Most of all, and especially when she saw the towering, storm-driven waves of Superior, she remembered what the big lake had taken from her and her family.

Paul, however, reveled in the water and the woods. Despite her protestations, he had taught her how to ski, and to snowshoe, and to ice fish, and to hunt grouse and deer, and to cast flies for bright brook trout.

The more Elizabeth had demurred in any new experience, the more Paul had insisted on it, constantly cajoling and goading her to try new things. And, the more he had drawn her out of her shell, the more she had brought a tiny amount of caution to his wild enthusiasm about everything at the same time; if for no other reason than out of concern for her, as if she were some tiny, fragile thing that needed his special, concerted protection.

And then, at some point after several months of dating, Paul and Elizabeth had simply merged. One entity, one being, for all the rest of time, Elizabeth had known then and still knew now.

Elizabeth's sisters and her mother had adored Paul, as did everyone he met, except felons. Her mother, however, had cautioned her strongly on the union. She still remembered the conversation as if it were yesterday, even though her mother had died fifteen years earlier; worn out much before her time by the hard work of providing for her fatherless children.

The words played back again in her mind now, as she remembered them. Elizabeth and her mother had been sitting in the living room of the small house that she had still shared with her mother at that time. Her sisters had long before married and had moved as far away from Ontonagon as possible. It was a fall night, after Paul had brought her back from a grouse hunt in the Ontonagon woods. There were six dressed birds that she and her mother would make for all of them the next day; pan-fried, with gravy, and mashed potatoes and rutabaga on the side, a meal that was still one of Paul's favorites.

It was quite late that night, Elizabeth recalled, long after her mother's normal bedtime. Elizabeth had been sitting on the sofa, wrapped both in a fleece bathrobe and in her dreamy thoughts of Paul's lips on hers, with his big hands on her breasts, on the porch during their goodbye. Her face was flushed, by both the cold air of the long day outside and by the barely constrained heat of her passion for the man.

Her mother was also in a bathrobe on the chair opposite, knitting, and glancing at Elizabeth knowingly on occasion. Her eyes were mostly focused on her work through her thick glasses, and her once blond hair, now gray, was in rollers.

"Elisabet", her mother had then said quietly, using the old Swedish pronunciation of her name, without looking up from her work; "Paul is a dear, good man, I know that. He loves you, that also is clear. And," she had said softly, raising her eyes finally to peer above her work at her daughter, "we both know that you are not getting any younger, my *Biti*."

Elizabeth had looked across the room at her mother. In her younger days, her mother had been a big woman, and strong. But now, as her mother sat in the chair holding her knitting, it had seemed to Elizabeth that the older woman was shrinking; collapsing into herself, like a mighty tree in the forest, a tree that had sheltered Elizabeth for all of her life but that was now finally giving way to age and disease.

"*Biti*," her mother had continued, her lined, pinched face tortured and with moisture forming at the corners of her eyes; "I love you more than life itself. Before I die I want to see you happy, even more so than you are tonight," she had said, with a small, knowing smile playing around her lips. "No one deserves it more than you, my dearest *Biti*."

"Mama?" Elizabeth had asked, warily, as if already suspecting where her mother was headed with this conversation.

"But," her mother had said, carefully, while shrugging her shoulders slightly and placing the knitting in her lap; "Paul's line of work is very dangerous, yes?"

"Well, yes, I suppose it can be," Elizabeth had said then, cautiously; she had never given it much thought. How could her Paul, her manly and apparently bulletproof Paul, ever be hurt by anything, she suddenly wondered? If anything, it would be Paul who did the hurting, if it came to it, she had thought, fiercely and proudly, her face flushing even more with the foreign thought.

"Mama, it is his job," Elizabeth had countered quietly, trying to subdue her emotions. "He is trained to do it, and as you know very well, he is more than capable of taking care of himself," she had continued, confidently.

"So I thought about your father," her mother had said sadly, nodding her gray head slowly. "The Bergstrom men had been fishermen since before the red Indians in this place were even living in bark wigwams."

Then, after a pause, her mother had continued. "Elisabet, I say this now only so that you will consider it. I love Paul, and you know that I do. And after this, I will close my mouth and give you both my blessing, and hold the children that you will bear him on my lap, and never say another word."

"I love you and your sisters deeply," Elizabeth's mother had continued, "and I always have. You have been my whole life. But, my *Biti*," she had then said, sternly, after a pause for effect; "you must know that a woman with children, children who have no father and no man to help provide for them, an older woman who can no longer hope to attract another man, that woman is worse than dead!"

"And yet, at the same time," she had added with a fatalistic shrug, in a burst of emotion as tears welled up in her old eyes that looked quickly upward towards the ceiling, "that woman is not permitted to die, for she must always live for her children!"

And then her mother had put down her knitting and stood, with the tears now running freely down her lined face. Refusing to be comforted, she had retired to her bedroom, while shaking her head and sobbing softly into her robe. Elizabeth had been left alone in the quiet room; a room suddenly filled with old, painful memories.

After their marriage, Elizabeth had followed Paul to all of the duty stations that were required of a bright, young Michigan State Policeman who was obviously on his way up the ladder. She bore their children, and she tried to keep some organization to their chaotic procession of moves and schools.

Nine years later, the state government gods had smiled on Paul. They had promoted him to Detective, to be stationed in his hometown of Houghton. Paul had been ecstatic about the promotion. Elizabeth had been much less so; but, ever the dutiful wife, she had said nothing and had simply packed up the family once again.

Elizabeth had quietly insisted upon one condition during their move to Houghton. They must live inland, to be close to work and shopping and schools in the hilly country surrounding Houghton, to minimize driving on icy roads, rather than living anywhere near the vastness of Lake Superior that surrounded much of Houghton and Keweenaw Counties.

Paul had quickly agreed since Elizabeth's concerns were eminently reasonable, as were all of her rare conditions. Paul had patrolled those same roads himself as a young trooper, and her issues made a lot of sense to him. And so they had come to live in this small, but ample, two-story house, in a quiet residential area off Sharon Avenue, on the high ground behind Michigan Technological University.

By her nature, and because of the daily demands on the busy mother of two, Elizabeth had never been much given to introspection. But in her heart, Elizabeth knew that her concerns were not about driving on icy roads, but instead were based on a much more primal fear, one that she hadn't shared with Paul. For, in fact, she hated and feared the big lake, the lake that had left its mark everywhere in this country.

Elizabeth hated Superior, for it had taken her father and had left her family destitute. She had to look at it every day during her girlhood in Ontonagon, where its icy waters had continually mocked her, indifferent to her loss. She feared its vastness, as a swimmer might fear deep water, where the bottom drops away and the depths become dark and unknowable.

One couldn't avoid Lake Superior completely, not in this country; not if you ever wanted to go anywhere else besides Houghton, Elizabeth knew, realistically. But, by living inland, at least she could take her children to school, or go shopping, or take her daily commute to her job at the

Houghton County courthouse, without seeing the vast blue sea and feeling the instant wrench in her heart at the thought of her father swallowed up in it.

At her age, Elizabeth was already beginning to lose some definition in her memories of her father, and of his appearance; like an old daguerreotype that, when viewed, lost a little bit of tint during each exposure to light. She desperately wanted to preserve the little that she had left of him.

With the cats fed, Elizabeth climbed the stairs to her bedroom to check on her husband before heading off to work at the courthouse. Paul had rolled in about three a.m. after a night of ice fishing on Lake Gogebic with his FBI acquaintance and occasional law enforcement partner, Sidney Hornberg. He was heading right back there later that day after a couple hours sleep, he had told her as he climbed into bed, before passing out with loud snores and with beer on his breath; the fishing was great!

Funny, she thought, as she opened the bedroom door and looked at the naked back of her husband, with the freckles splayed across the shoulders and the tousled blond hair of the back of his head; there weren't any fish in the fridge when she had looked this morning. She hadn't even known that the city boy, Hornberg, even liked ice fishing! Paul was now in a deep sleep, but he would awaken instantly and dress like an automaton as soon as the alarm on his side of the bed went off, having been conditioned by years of police work.

That was just like her Paul, Elizabeth thought affectionately, as she admired his broad, muscular back: drop everything at a moment's notice, and spend the night on a frozen lake with a casual friend, all for the sake of a few fish! "I'm Peter Pan, I don't want to grow up, I won't grow up!"— that could have been her husband's theme, she thought fondly, as he stirred in his sleep, the muscles in his naked back rippling.

To the rest of the world, Paul Adams might be a seasoned and hardened police professional, Elizabeth reflected; but to his wife, he was still a twenty-four year old state police rookie with a golden glow about him, a young man with boundless enthusiasm for everything that life had to offer. He belonged in this country, she knew, for he would always be a little wild, like the woodland things that resist domestication.

As she looked down on her husband, Elizabeth pinched an inch of skin with her fingers from beneath the triceps in her upper left arm and frowned. It just wasn't fair, she thought indignantly, as she turned to look at the streaks of gray in her short blond hair in the mirror above the dresser. At fifty-four years of age, she was starting to look like a smaller version of her mother, but at fifty, Paul hadn't aged a day after twenty-six years of marriage! Four years age difference shouldn't be that obvious, she sniffed dejectedly.

Oh sure, she thought jealously, if you looked closely at Paul's face you could see the creases starting to form beneath his eyes, creases set in a face that was turning leathery after years of exposure to the sun. But still, that body; my God, that body! After all the years, Elizabeth still thrilled to her man's touch in the quiet nights in their bedroom.

But something was bothering Paul, Elizabeth knew; something that had started some time earlier, on that night when a heavy concussion west towards Ontonagon, out on the big lake, had rattled the windows of their Houghton home, along with most of the other windows in this part of the Upper Peninsula. A ship's hold, or something like that, she recalled reading.

Even the girls had noticed that their dad had seemed more distracted and preoccupied than usual, even though he hadn't said anything. Not that he ever did, Elizabeth knew from long experience. Her husband was a professional police officer who did not bring his problems home with him, one who was content to be a doting dad and a loving husband away from work. That is, when he wasn't hunting, fishing, or up to no good with his chums, she thought, wryly and affectionately.

What an explosion on a ship in the middle of Lake Superior could possibly have to do with the Michigan State Police, Elizabeth could not fathom, and Paul had been no help in helping her to connect the dots. But lately, his work hours had been very long, due no doubt to the incredible amount of violence in his district that seemed to be in the evening papers each evening, violence completely out of character for the western Upper Peninsula.

The recent mass murder of hunters down by Rousseau seemed to have particularly shaken Paul. So, she thought resignedly, as she quietly closed the door to the bedroom and made her way back down the stairs to begin her daily commute to the Houghton County courthouse, if freezing his lovely butt off on a frozen lake would help him put aside whatever it was that was bothering him, if only for a few hours, then she and the girls would be all for it.

Elizabeth closed the front door behind her and walked across the icy driveway to her small Ford SUV. After starting the car, she let it idle to warm up, while she got out to scrape the nightly accumulation of frost from her windshield.

As she worked, Elizabeth Bergstrom-Adams could not escape a nagging feeling, a sense of unease that was like a dull ache, far behind her eyes; a feeling that, in some unknowable way, Lake Superior would again have a major impact on her and her family's lives. She could see in the breaking dawn that the sky was dark and overcast.

Elizabeth could feel that the wind was picking up from the northwest, off the big lake, with a bite of cold moisture to it as it struck her cheek. She shuddered briefly. It would be a stormy day.

CHAPTER 12

▼

It was mid-morning. Sidney Hornberg and Paul Adams were retracing the same route west that they had taken the night before on their ice fishing expedition to Lake Gogebic, on State Highway M-28. Adams was at the wheel of an unmarked Chevrolet Tahoe that he had commandeered from the State Police motor pool. The western horizon was black with the ominous clouds of an approaching storm; huge, billowing clouds, standing out from the backdrop of sky before them like raised welts on a background of purple bruises, scarring the virgin white landscape before them.

The weather forecast had predicted major snowfall for the afternoon hours. It had lent impetus to their mission since, as Adams had commented dourly, even a small amount of snow on top of what was already on the ground would make unplowed back roads impassable, even for the big police SUV that they were now riding in. This might be the only chance they would have, Adams had continued darkly, to help this mysterious Ukrainian physicist, Doctor Sergei Lysenko, a man whom they had never met and who was the apparent focus of all of these latest terrible events, remain alive—if it was even still possible at this point, he had added, morosely.

Hornberg briefly reflected on the past few hours, as the miles passed quietly in the big police SUV on its westerly route, since Adams, uncharacteristically, seemed to be in little mood for conversation this morning. The hardwoods, interspersed here and there with hemlock, cedar, and the occasional white pine, stood out starkly against the wintry backdrop; black, skeletal shapes against the rolling terrain, shapes that bordered his thoughts, as they flashed through his mind, like old daguerreotype picture frames.

Hornberg had met his wife, Emma, in their kitchen that same morning as he had groped about in the cupboard for a coffee cup. He had barely been able to see properly, having had only a few hours sleep; thanks to his friend, Paul Adams, and their ice fishing excursion of the previous night.

As Adams had predicted, the few small walleye fillets that she had discovered in her refrigerator that morning, prepared with as much care as Adams had been able to muster after a long night on the ice and after several beers at Jumpy's, had delighted Emma. Hornberg's wife was an Upper Peninsula native who was no stranger to either worm dirt or fish parts. Could it be, she had teased Hornberg, with a small, coy smile on her face and her pride in his sudden and surprising cultural reformation readily obvious, that her city boy, FBI agent husband, Sidney, was going native?

Galvanized, as her gaze fell lovingly on the translucent fish fillets in the shallow glass dish in her hands and as her mind mentally transmuted them into some type of delectable piscatorial cuisine, accompanied by a special tartar sauce and a fresh vegetable, Hornberg's wife had then launched excitedly into a rambling and well-practiced re-telling of her girlhood. She had been a tomboy, she always said, as the oft-told tale unfolded. Hornberg unconsciously ticked off the familiar, well-remembered bookmarks of the story as she spoke.

Hornberg had heard it all before, many times, over the years: the stories of her father and her favorite Finnish uncles; and old boats, and wooden docks, and ruined cabins falling down; and lily pads and frogs; and sunny days spent in braids and bib overalls; and cane poles held by delighted little girls, with cork floats suspending minnows and worms in small lakes for bass, pike, walleyes, and panfish. This was all long before conformity, education, and aspiration had rendered such youthful pastimes as merely frivolous for a socially prominent young woman of the Marquette community, his wife would say, and oh, how she missed it! So the story always ended, on a wistful and plaintive note, and always accompanied by a pensive expression on his wife's aging, but still beautiful, face.

Hornberg had then smiled fondly and nodded vacantly, as he always did when this particular story was told. But in truth, he had barely heard his wife as she babbled on animatedly in the early morning hours about times long gone. His mind was still fuzzy from lack of sleep, and it was in a far darker place, with a vague trepidation of events to come.

They were getting on in years, Hornberg realized, both he and his wife. They were two people, now slightly more than middle-aged, who had somehow managed to fall together after all their youth and their passion had been spent; lives spent mostly on life pursuits that had not particularly benefited either of them. Living in the past now seemed to be more normal than not for both of them, Hornberg reflected, somewhat bitterly.

Sidney Hornberg had finally become old enough and wise enough to recognize his wife's wistful recollections as the sad refrain of their collective generational anthem, that of the 'Baby Boomers'. Not for them the clean, crisp deaths of their parents, dead before their natural times from either world war or from the pesticides and industrial advances that had both benefited and doomed them at the same time, Hornberg knew now. No, his generation was destined to wallow in semi-affluence, self-pity, and angst until some new and previously unknown cancer or other some danger claimed it; dangers which previous generations had never lived long enough to have to deal with.

Hornberg's heart ached, riding now in the big police SUV and remembering the tone of his wife's voice as she repeated the story of her youth; a youth that he had never known nor shared, and could not possibly comprehend, because of their very different backgrounds. And when he had left the house, before walking to the deli on the corner in his neighborhood in Marquette to meet Paul Adams, he had held her closely for a very long time; silently, trying to impress her memory on the very fiber of his being, as if he might never see her again.

The two men's fictitious excuses for missing work that morning had been accepted with only slightly sarcastic comments from their co-workers. Being over-served in a tavern in the Upper Peninsula happened occasionally to even normally conservative police officials, especially after spending a cold night ice fishing in the middle of a huge frozen lake.

By the time that they had turned south at the community of Bruce Crossing for the run to Watersmeet, Adams had finally begun talking again. He had then given Hornberg a brief history of their destination, the Sylvania Wilderness.

At one time, Adams had told him knowledgably, the entire eighteen thousand acre collection of lakes and old growth hardwoods of the Sylvania had been the personal playpen of an association of some of the richest industrial moguls in the Midwest, a group known as the 'Sylvania Club'. They had built lodges, cabins, and boathouses on all of the largest lakes in the tract, and then they had built roads, good macadam roads, to connect them all.

The Sylvania Club had no interest in logging their beautiful, pristine forest, Adams had told him. Having no need for the income, the rich industrialists had used it only for hunting, fishing, relaxing, and politicking with their peers. Presidents, congressmen, judges, and influential industrialists and journalists had been among their many grateful guests.

Ownership, Adams continued, had changed hands several times over the years. In 1967 the United States Forest Service had purchased the land, opening it to the public for the first time. All buildings had been removed from the property. The good roads were bulldozed up, and the vast tract was managed as a special recreation area for the next twenty years until 1987, when it was finally designated a Federal Wilderness Area.

At the present, Adams had explained, tough recreational regulations were rigidly enforced for all visitors to the Wilderness, regulations that were designed to ensure that man's touch on this special place was as light as possible. Even Forest Service personnel, Adams added with a wicked chuckle, had to walk or paddle a canoe into back country areas that needed maintenance and then had to use an axe, a bucksaw, or a shovel when they got there, since any wheeled vehicles, and all motorized equipment, were strictly prohibited in the Wilderness. The long dead industrialists, those icons of American industry and the original owners, would have found this all very amusing and ironic, Adams had merrily asserted.

Hornberg, however, his mood suddenly as dark as the western horizon, was no longer in a condition to be amused by Adams' light banter, even now that the man was his usual chatty self again. They had just passed through a tiny community that was no bigger than a speed bump on the south-bound road. It was called Paulding, a tiny crossroads consisting of no more than a curve in the road, a bar, a small bridge, and a country store.

Vivid memories now flooded back to Hornberg. A few days previously, he had regained consciousness on that same country store's step with a bad taste in his mouth, blindfolded and bundled in a sleeping bag, and with his hands duct-taped behind him.

The nightmare of 'Gregor' was immediately with Hornberg again as he remembered those awful events. Someway, somehow, he thought passionately, as the ringing started again in his ears, if it's the last thing I ever do as an FBI agent, that sick bastard, Gregor, has to die!

Hornberg could barely hear Adams now as they traveled down the highway, so loud was the ringing in his ears, as the rage again enveloped him. His career, his wife, his personal life, and his very existence were now toys that both his superiors and his enemies were playing with. Someone, he vowed abstractly, would surely pay, and pay dearly.

Alone in his black thoughts, Hornberg railed at his perceived perversities of the professional life he had led. His career, earnestly and devotedly spent in government service with the Federal Bureau of Investigation, had all been crap, he thought suddenly, in a flash of bitter self-revelation; one big, spasmodic cramp in his personal journey of life. He had been trained to protect lives, he reflected ironically, but it seemed to him now that only by taking another life, the life of this 'Gregor' monster, could he hope for any personal redemption or any control at all over his own destiny.

With effort, Hornberg concentrated on his respiration. His occasional heart palpitations had begun again, but now they quickly diminished as he forced himself away from his black thoughts. Nothing I do consciously seems to come to any good, he thought wryly, as if in some sudden, temporarily insane insight; unconscious, involuntary actions, like breathing, seem to be the only things that I can do very well anymore.

Glancing at Adams behind the wheel, Hornberg saw that the big state police detective had thankfully not noticed his brief lapse into lunacy, for he was still chatting away to no one in particular, like some overly enthusiastic tour guide. Paul just never knows when to quit, Hornberg thought, as he looked at his younger professional friend with affection; God, to be his age again, still having all that energy!

Hornberg's moments of bitter introspection quickly passed, and in short order the Lac Vieux Desert casino jumped up out of the trees on their left hand. Absently, Hornberg noted well over two hundred cars in the big parking lot already at this early hour, with many of the vehicles sporting Wisconsin license plates. Mighty early in the day to be gambling, folks, he thought, vaguely and judgmentally.

Hornberg's mind was freewheeling, trying to put the bad thoughts behind him, as his eyes briefly caught the 'Dancing Eagles' logo on the garish roadside sign. It registered an unanswered question, for the symbolism was foreign to his logical policeman's brain.

Hornberg had never been a gambler, and the predilection of lonely old people and foolish young people alike to squander their funds in Upper Peninsula Indian casinos had always been a source of continuous amazement to him. But even in his dark mood, Hornberg was forced to briefly laugh at himself, an abrupt, braying sound that caused Adams to glance at him quickly in surprise. Hornberg did not bother trying to explain the source of his amusement to his friend. I am possibly about to get my ass shot off and here I am, worried about what other people do with their money, he derided himself, mockingly.

As they entered the small town of Watersmeet, the Home of the Nimrods, as the sign proclaimed, Adams turned their vehicle west on U.S. Highway 2 for only a few miles and then turned south again on a blacktopped county road. They were close now, Adams explained excitedly.

After only a few miles on the county road, the big police SUV pulled into a turn-off where directed by a Forest Service sign. They drove past a snow-covered A-frame building that served as the access and entrance station to the Sylvania Wilderness. Then, in four-wheel drive, the vehicle burrowed into the twelve inches of old snow that covered the remainder of the unplowed road past that point. The snow barely slowed the big Tahoe as it powered down the macadam forest road.

"My old man used to bring me and my brothers in here all the time while we were growing up," Adams explained, with a wistful expression on his face as he reminisced about his lumberman father, long since dead from a logging accident. "It's been quite a while since I've had a reason to come back," he said, somberly.

"I used to know this Sylvania country like the back of my hand," Adams continued animatedly, waving his arm to encompass the vista. "We hunted and fished all over, off of the forest roads, all the way to Marenisco, back before they put in the medium-security state prison there. Logging, landfills, and prisons," he recited sadly; "they're about the only growth opportunities we have left up here. Most of the mining, farming, and small industries died out in the U.P. long ago."

"I guess that Dad figured that all of this country is going to be suburban Green Bay or Wausau, someday," Adams continued, in a subdued tone, "and he wanted us kids to remember the way it used to be, or at least as close as he could get us to it, anyway." Adams now fell silent, concentrating on his driving.

The big SUV drove slowly through the white snow lying on the floor of the dark tunnel of old-growth hardwoods. The crisp snow made a squeaking sound whenever the tires changed direction slightly. The freshening wind blew small clumps of snow from the boughs of the trees that surrounded them into their path. Tiny ice crystals rattled off the windshield like birdshot.

"Weather's rolling in now, Sid," Adams said, glancing quickly above the steering column at the small sliver of sky that was visible through the huge hardwoods of the Sylvania. "But," he continued, matter-of-factly, as if he were on just another outdoor excursion, "if this isn't a wild goose chase, at least whoever is in here is going to have a hard time seeing us coming."

After just a few miles of travel through deserted campgrounds, with closed gates and wooden, brown-and-gold signs mounded high with snow, Adams pulled the big SUV into a large parking area that overlooked a large, stone-and-mortar building set against the shore of a long lake, a lake that disappeared into the east as the quickening weather obscured its outline. Hornberg glanced at a large wooden sign that was still legible beneath its covering of snow; 'Clark Lake Day Use Area', the sign proclaimed. Hornberg was incredulous.

"Paul, you're not going to try to tell me that there is a secret research lab in a Forest Service picnic area, are you?" Hornberg asked, with disbelief written across his face.

"No, Sid," Adams answered, with a low, mirthless chuckle. "This is just the back way in. The normal access is through a locked gate off the county road that we drove in on. They'll have surveillance on that."

"I figure that they haven't bothered with the woods approaches, since there isn't supposed to be anyone in here this time of year," Adams explained, logically. "Plus, before the final winter freeze, this way is swampy and tough to get through."

While Hornberg continued to consider the sanity of their mission in the quickening storm, he and Adams exited the big SUV and closed the side doors quietly. They then waded through the twelve inches of old snow to the rear of the Tahoe, dropped the tailgate, and then sat on it as they donned their gear: lightweight, roomy undergarments above their street clothes; knee-high waterproof boots; bullet-resistant Kelvar vests; followed by insulated, white-and-brown camouflage coveralls, balaclavas, hoods, and gloves.

Adams then opened a weapons case and extracted a Colt M4A1 assault rifle. He slapped in a thirty round magazine loaded with 5.56 millimeter NATO rounds and set it carefully aside, after checking to ensure that the safety was on. After sliding several extra magazines into a side pocket of his coveralls, Adams opened a separate weapons case and withdrew a similar M4A1 assault rifle, but one with an unusual, bulky device mounted atop the weapon forward of its iron sights. He then passed the weapon to Hornberg, along with several magazines of ammunition.

"You get the new toy, Sid," Adams commented with a slight smile, his face framed and pinched by his pulled-down balaclava. "Most of the State Police haven't even seen this yet, let alone shoot it. That little beauty on top is a combination thermal imaging device and 4X scope", he explained, with a rapt expression; "it works in daylight, nighttime, anytime," he continued, in a voice filled with professional admiration. "Rain, snow, fog, it doesn't matter; if it's got a heat signature, this thing will tell you what the guy had on his pizza last night to a distance of five hundred feet. I thought that it might come in handy, today of all days", Adams explained, dourly.

Adams then quickly explained the operation of the device to Hornberg, pointing to each tiny switch and button and explaining its function, as the FBI man held the weapon in front of him. Hornberg then briefly practiced by scanning the tree line and the lakeshore and the nearby figure of Adams with the unloaded weapon. He noted with considerable amazement the startlingly stark white images against the darker white and gray backdrop of the surrounding snow covered landscape of even the tiniest creatures that were still active on this winter day, the Canada jays and the red squirrels.

Nodding his head in satisfaction, Hornberg inserted a magazine into the carbine and checked the safety. With Adams in the lead, the two men then set off down the snow-covered shoreline path along Clark Lake towards a high hardwood ridge in the distance, now barely visible through the swirling snow.

After only a few hundred yards, with Hornberg carefully walking in Adams' boot tracks, the path that they were quietly following abruptly dropped into a slight depression. At the bottom of the depression, the outlet creek of Clark Lake flowed into a boggy slough of a smaller lake to the west, a lake that was noticeably lower in elevation. The little creek looked like a small, black-and-silver, ice-fringed scar as it zigzagged across the snowy background, bisecting cattails and skirting around snow-covered hummocks.

Adams waited until Hornberg had pulled abreast of him. "This is Helen Lake", Adams said, in a low voice, with his free hand cupped to Hornberg's ear, pointing to the smaller lake. "Like I said before, I'm betting that they don't have surveillance on this end. They would have had no reason to have it here while the water was open."

"The research station sits up on that ridge in front of us", Adams continued quietly, as he indicated the higher ground to the south. "We'll follow the shoreline until we get to that hemlock point," he said, gesturing vaguely at a dark mass on the western horizon that Hornberg could barely see through the snow that was now falling steadily. "We'll haul out there. We should be able to stay under cover and check the place out thoroughly from there. Stay in my tracks, and don't step on any wet spots!" Adams cautioned, as he set off through the bog.

The two men carefully and cautiously made their way westward along the boggy shoreline of the small lake, one behind the other, for several hundred yards. The snow was falling more heavily now. It splashed against their clothing and into their covered faces like big, wet, white cotton wads, but at the same time, it was still interspersed with occasional small, icy pellets.

Finally, when they had reached a slightly higher, evergreen-covered point, Adams left the lake ice and carefully worked his way up the slight slope. Hornberg followed, and soon they were sheltered from the storm around them beneath the boughs of massive, old-growth hemlock trees.

The air was quiet and calm beneath the old giants. Even the ground was mostly still bare, with the bulk of the old snow having been captured by the permanently green canopy above them. As Hornberg looked around him while he followed Adams through the hemlock grove, he saw wires running everywhere, with instruments having no clear purpose mounted to the trunks of several of the hemlocks and inserted into the frozen ground at various locations.

Adams made his way carefully through the hemlock grove until he reached a deadfall at its edge, one that overlooked a small frozen bay of the lake and gave a view of a high hardwood ridge on the other side. Hornberg joined him behind the deadfall. Snow was falling heavily now. It obscured their view of the ridge, across the mostly open hardwoods and frozen lake surface that separated them, like a thick gauze curtain drawn across the scene from their sheltered location below the hemlocks.

"That's it, the Helen Lake Flux Tower," Adams said, in a whisper, as he pointed to a tall, barely visible, manmade structure on the ridge, a metal tower that reached above the tops of the tallest of the old hardwoods that surrounded it. "Pretty innocuous-looking, eh?"

"I would say," Hornberg agreed, returning the whisper, as he scanned the ridge with his weapon. He could clearly see the sharp white outlines of heat sources that appeared to be power supplies in metal enclosures, for the instruments that littered the snowy landscape and that were mounted on the big trees in all directions. But except for these, the surroundings were cold and bare and apparently devoid of life. "Looks like it's just what it's been advertised to be, Paul," Hornberg said, doubtfully, "some sort of tree research project."

"Yeah, it's probably just a wild goose chase, like I said, me and my hyperactive imagination," Adams whispered back, shaking his head. "But as long as we're here, let's give it a while and see if anything happens," he continued quietly. Hornberg agreed silently with a quick nod.

The minutes stretched into nearly an hour. The snow was falling even more heavily now. It was beginning to accumulate on even the previously bare ground beneath their sheltering hemlocks. Their faint tracks into the place had been completely obliterated by this time. It'll be a fun drive home tonight, Hornberg thought bleakly, as he watched the hardwoods in front of him filling up at the rate of an inch an hour.

Hornberg was already beginning to cramp up behind the deadfall, unaccustomed to the uncomfortable position. He was moving only occasionally, to sweep the ridge with the thermal imager on his weapon. Adams, however, still kneeled motionless, with his focus fixed on the opposite ridge, as the snow began to mound up on his insulated, camouflaged features; like a long-practiced hunter awaiting his prey.

And suddenly, they were there. Hornberg had just begun a routine sweep of the ridge with the thermal device on his weapon when he saw them through the scope; the clear white outlines of two human figures, making their way across the ridge towards their position from the direction of the entrance two-track.

"We've got company," Hornberg whispered to Adams, pointing in the direction of the figures. Adams squinted through the falling snow until he caught the men's motion through the trees, and then he nodded, silently.

"What do you want to bet that it's our spook friends?" Adams asked, whispering towards Hornberg.

"No bet," Hornberg responded, as he followed the progress of the two figures through the thermal imaging scope.

They continued to watch as the two men walked through the blowing snow, confidently, as if they knew the way. At last, they reached the steep slope opposite them that fell away to the small frozen bay of Helen Lake. They stopped at an old, snow covered hemlock stump. The lead figure then removed a glove and began to jab at the stump with a finger, a series of jabs interspersed with pauses, as if he were entering a code.

Several moments passed. Then the, steep, snowy hillside across from them silently slid towards them on its hydraulic slides, revealing the cavernous maw of the bunker behind it with its eerie red glow. The two figures entered the bunker, and it swallowed them up into its redness. Then the hillside slid into itself again, leaving all as it had been before; a landscape that was silent, cold, and apparently lifeless, in a raging snowstorm that muted everything. Hornberg and Adams looked at each other in complete astonishment.

Adams said it for both of them, simply and quietly, in a bewildered voice: "Well, I'll be dipped in shit!"

*   *   *   *

Inside the comfortable, red-lit bunker, Bruce Wilton of the Directorate of Operations for the Central Intelligence Agency and Colonel Frank Wenzel, of the Office of the Deputy Chief of Staff, Intelligence-G2, United States Army were shaking the snow from their overcoats as they were approached by the big Indian. "So, Loonsfoot, where is 'The Package'?" asked Wilton tersely.

"At the shooting gallery, as usual," responded Agent Thomas Loonsfoot, in a flat monotone. "Working, as usual", he continued, his face expressionless.

"And the maintenance crew?" queried Wenzel.

"I released them this morning, before the storm. We are alone here at present," Loonsfoot replied dispassionately.

"Excellent!" replied Wilton, in a low voice, as he hung his wet coat on a rack. They didn't need any unnecessary complication, and now there wouldn't be, since the Ukrainian didn't understand much English. Turning to face Loonsfoot, Wilton locked the big man's eyes with his own while facing upward slightly; the Indian was six inches taller than himself.

"Agent Loonsfoot," Wilton continued in a quiet, conspiratorial tone, with a quick glance towards Colonel Wenzel; "I've received our final directions from 'Thor', and it is now time to proceed with the plan. Do you remember your instructions?" he demanded of the Indian, brusquely.

"Yes, sir," Loonsfoot replied, like an automaton, with no hint of emotion in his voice. He had been expecting this very question for some time now.

The Central Intelligence Agency's experts had carefully coached Loonsfoot for many months, well before they had taken 'The Package' from his native Ukraine and before Loonsfoot had been made his keeper. Loonsfoot's top-secret clearance, his physical prowess, and his knowledge of the local terrain had made him the obvious choice for this regrettable business. Such was the nature of covert intelligence in this day and age that even the United States, its moral imperatives aside, had to engage in the occasional 'wet work', they had emphasized to Loonsfoot.

Loonsfoot's CIA superiors had made these very obvious facts abundantly clear to him, repeatedly. Constant psychological vetting had guaranteed that Agent Thomas Loonsfoot would carry out his duty to his sovereign nation.

It had naturally always been assumed by the Agency that they and the Indian agent were discussing the identically same sovereign nation, since they had little experience with Native American priorities in general. The Federal men could not have comprehended that it might have registered somewhat differently to Loonsfoot, who was an Ojibwa man.

Now, the plan Loonsfoot had been coached in was to play out. Per his standing instructions, Loonsfoot would take the pale Ukrainian physicist, Doctor Sergei Lysenko, far into the Sylvania backcountry on this winter day and eliminate him; in as humane a manner as possible, Loonsfoot had been reminded on several occasions. He would then conceal the body in such a manner so as it would never be found; in this National Wilderness, an area guaranteed by Federal statute to never see so much as a shovel full of dirt turned over, in order to preserve its pristine wildness. The high northern hardwoods of this wild country would hide Doctor Lysenko forever. He would have vanished as if he had never existed.

Having eliminated the physicist, Loonsfoot would then return to the Helen Lake bunker and set the timed charges. These would cause an explosion that would obliterate the bunker and all traces of what had transpired there after he, Agent Loonsfoot, was well away. Then, after leaving the Sylvania, he was to depart the Watersmeet area permanently and vanish into the large Ojibwa population of Minnesota, until such a time as he was recalled by the Agency by a pre-arranged electronic message for a future assignment.

After asking a few perfunctory questions, Wilton and Wenzel had satisfied themselves that Agent Thomas Loonsfoot still understood his instructions and that he would still carry out his assignment as he had been programmed. After the two men had struggled back into their wet coats, Wilton pushed the button on a hydraulic controller next to the bunker door. This caused the snowy hillside that fell down into the small bay of the lake to separate once again as the hydraulic door slid open, exposing the warm, red internals of the bunker to the raging snowstorm outside.

With a final, fraternal wave to the big Indian, the two Federal intelligence agents walked out into the cold, snow-filled evening air of the Sylvania Wilderness. Of the three CIA men present, only they knew that there was no timing feature on the explosive charges that lined the internal walls of the Helen Lake bunker. The explosion would occur as soon as Agent Thomas Loonsfoot attempted to set the timing device, following his elimination of 'The Package'.

*   *   *   *

Behind the deadfall in the hemlock grove, Hornberg and Adams watched through the driving snow as the hillside opened its gaping red maw once again and disgorged the two familiar men. They had seen them turn and wave to someone unseen within the bunker, before they had ascended the steep slope while the hillside closed behind them. It continued to snow furiously.

"Now what?" asked Adams, quietly into the snowy void, as he watched the two figures retreating towards the two-track that was the entrance to the research facility.

"Now, it gets complicated," Hornberg replied, grimly.

Out of habit, a habit learned long before in a foreign land in a much younger body, in another war, Hornberg had begun to scan their back trail with the thermal imaging device mounted on his weapon. He had just seen two additional human figures behind them on the high hardwood ridge that overlooked the hemlock grove that sheltered them. The two figures were not moving. Their thermal images stood out bright white among the dark surrounding trees, within easy rifle range.

"We've got more company behind us, Paul," Hornberg whispered. "Two men, and they seem to know approximately where we are."

"Shit!" exploded Adams, the expletive spitted through clenched teeth. "Maybe the spooks had surveillance back there after all! We had better get small!"

With that, both Adams and Hornberg crabbed around the dead tree and reversed their position to the bunker side of the deadfall, to place it between them and the new threat. As they scrambled to get as low to the ground as possible, they did not hear the muted, double *pop-pop, pop-pop,* noise that came from the two-track entrance to the research facility on the ridge behind them; for the heavy snow was obscuring everything, including sound.

As he and Adams crouched behind the deadfall, Hornberg found a small crotch in the dead hemlock that permitted him a view towards the two strangers on the ridge. He watched through the imager while they got down into a prone, fighting position and then crept slowly towards their woody barricade, aggressively. Their thermal images were intermittent behind the heavy cover. Soon, the two sets of men were within hailing distance, but they were still invisible to each other with their naked eyes through the driving snow.

A sudden burst of automatic rifle fire from the two on the ridge caused Hornberg and Adams to cringe and flatten to the frozen ground. Snow and bits of wood and bark rained down on them as the bullets tore through the deadfall above their heads.

For several moments all was quiet, while Hornberg and Adams quietly assured each other that neither had been hit. And then, incredulously, they both heard the loud, shouted voice above the raging tumult: "Hallooo, Sidney! This is Gregor! We meet again, yes?"

Hornberg and Adams looked at each other in brief astonishment. Then they inched towards each other, as low to the ground as possible, until they were touching. "Is that him, Sid?" Adams whispered into Hornberg's ear.

"Sure sounds like him," Hornberg whispered back. "What now?"

"If he's talking, he's not shooting," Adams answered, grimly. "They've got us pretty well pinned down here, Sid. Our one chance is to try to flank them, or we're dead. Try to keep him talking, if you can. I'll try to work my way around them on the right, up the ridge. Can you give me a landmark?" he whispered urgently in Hornberg's ear.

Hornberg stuck his weapon through the small crotch in the dead hemlock that he had used previously and scanned their attackers' position on the ridge. The thermal image of the little that was exposed of each man was small, but distinct.

"There's a clump of three small hardwoods on the ridge at twelve o'clock, range fifty yards," Hornberg informed Adams tersely. "There's a man on each side of that clump about ten feet way from it, behind a little rise."

Adams carefully peered through the deadfall until he located the hardwoods through the swirling snow, and then he focused on it for several moments, trying to memorize the exact location. "Got it", he said finally. "Okay, Sid, I'm gone. Keep them talking. Shoot back if they shoot at you, keep them where they are right now!" And with that, Adams was off, crabbing to the right of the deadfall ever so slowly, trying to take advantage of every branch, every twig, anything that could provide cover.

"So Gregor, just how did you know where we were?" Hornberg yelled from behind the deadfall, in honest puzzlement. The stiff breeze behind him carried his voice up the ridge, mingling it with the driving snow.

"How is that little cut on the back of your neck from the last time we met, Sidney?" Gregor shouted vaguely in reply. "No discomfort, I hope?"

Hornberg remembered the small scratch clearly from the physical exam following his abduction to Rousseau by Gregor, on the night that they had drunk the corn liquor in the dead men's cabin. It had been the only mark on him after a night of being handled by his abductors. At the time, he had simply assumed that he'd been bumped against something sharp. Hornberg now rubbed his neck absently, through the wetness left by the damp snow on his camouflage coveralls.

"The technology we have today is wonderful," Gregor shouted cheerfully from up on the ridge, as Hornberg glanced in Adams' direction to check his progress. Adams was barely ten yards from the deadfall, moving very carefully and deliberately and almost painfully slowly.

"We implanted you with a very tiny radio-frequency identification transponder, about the size of a grain of rice," Gregor continued, loudly and matter-of-factly. "The satellite links aren't so good yet, and we have fewer of them flying nowadays", he shouted into the snow, almost apologetically. "But still, we have been able to track you to within a kilometer or so, which is more than good enough for our purposes. We even followed you on your ice fishing excursion last night!" Gregor yelled merrily into the snowy night, as if teasing a close colleague. "*Blyaha muha*, you Americans are crazy!"

Hornberg absorbed this information as if struck dumb. 'Bird on a wire'; 'canary in a cage'; 'white rat'; the mental images flew about his mind as he searched frantically for Adams, who was now out of view.

Ever since Rousseau, he'd been a walking, talking, location beacon, a toy for this Russian asshole, Hornberg now realized belatedly. He had instantly recognized the slang expression that Gregor had shouted down from the ridge, from years of youthful experience with various Russian criminal elements.

"Just what the fuck do you want, Gregor?" Hornberg shouted into the wind from behind the deadfall, as he scanned to the right with the thermal imager on his weapon. He had Adams now; he was well up the ridge, almost to the same level as their attackers.

"What we have always wanted, Sidney," came the shouted answer. "We want our man back. We knew that if we gave you enough slack line, you would eventually lead us to him. Like a big fish, yes?" Gregor shouted, as if sharing a professional confidence. The answer came as no surprise to Hornberg.

"You are not out here tonight with your policeman friend, in this terrible weather, hunting the numerous white rabbits of this area, no?" Gregor yelled, sarcastically, into the wind from the ridge. "I think not. Is this where you are keeping our Doctor Lysenko?" he demanded, abruptly. Hornberg offered no reply.

"Listen, Sidney," Gregor shouted down the ridge, as if to a confidant. "It is not necessary for you and your policeman friend, or anyone else, to die on this night. This Lysenko is nothing to you! Let us have him. We shall take both him and our nuclear devices out of your country and leave you in peace, so that you can die in your beds as old men," the Russian argued. "You and I, Sidney, we have both seen enough of death in our lifetimes, I think," Gregor shouted, reasonably.

Hornberg braced himself behind the deadfall, knowing that Adams must have reached a shooting position by this time. And then, suddenly, Adams was on his feet behind a large yellow birch tree, emptying his thirty-round magazine into the attackers' positions in a fraction of a second. The muzzle flashes of his weapon were a solid column of fire, so close were the rounds to each other amid the large swirling snowflakes on the ridge, while the sounds were muted by the storm.

A yelp of pain from his target filled the sudden silence as Adams dropped behind the yellow birch to reload. Then Hornberg stood up from behind the deadfall and also emptied his weapon in the general direction of the attackers. His aim was poor, since the thermal imaging scope on his carbine had now been rendered useless by his own muzzle flashes.

Hornberg had just dropped back behind the deadfall, fumbling in his coveralls for another magazine, when Adams stood to continue the assault. Hornberg then saw, in horror, that Adams was caught in crossfire from the bunker area. The staccato bursts from two automatic weapons, at point blank range behind him, seemed to almost cut Adams in half. He pitched forward at the waist, with his backbone shattered, from behind the yellow birch onto the ground of the snowy ridge, like a broken rag doll.

Hornberg stood and faced back grimly towards the new threat. Then he too was caught in crossfire from the same two weapons, and a line of fire stitched across his chest. Several slugs punched into the Kelvar vest and knocked him backwards into the branches of the deadfall, completely senseless. Unconsciousness quickly claimed Hornberg, enveloping him in a blackness that was even darker than the snowy night around him.

*   *   *   *

Inside the bunker, the surveillance camera that monitored the area in front of the hydraulic entrance door told Agent Thomas Loonsfoot all he needed to know: there was a firefight going on, right outside the bunker. Muzzle flashes were spread all over the edge of the hemlock grove, across the small frozen bay that lay at the foot of the bunker. There would be no way out in that direction. Time for 'Plan B', he thought grimly.

It had taken Loonsfoot several months, but he had finally found what he had been sure must be part of the original bunker construction: an escape hatch at the borehole end of the bunker, or the 'shooting gallery', as Loonsfoot thought of it. Some faceless Federal engineer had obviously provided the escape hatch, in slavish compliance to an engineering code that required an alternate exit route in the event of failure of the hydraulic entrance door, or a fire, or toxic fumes within the bunker. But it had then been sacrificed to the priority of providing adequate cooling for the myriad power supplies, laser devices and computers that were part of Doctor Lysenko's tools of the trade, and it had been completely covered over by ventilation ductwork. Careful searching, during better weather, had shown that the exit of the escape hatch was on the opposite side of the ridge of old hardwoods, buried beneath leaf litter.

Loonsfoot hurried towards the borehole with a pry bar in his hand, a tool that he had been keeping for just such an emergency. Shouting to the pale Ukrainian physicist that he needed to dress, and dress warmly, he then snapped open a stepladder beneath a section of overhead ventilation supplies and attacked the ductwork with the pry bar.

While the puzzled scientist did not fully comprehend all of Loonsfoot's words, the urgency in the big Indian's actions more than adequately conveyed their meaning to Lysenko. Shutting down the scientific equipment that he was using, Lysenko ran to an adjacent anteroom and got into his winter gear, while pieces of galvanized ductwork, both large and small, rained down onto the floor of the bunker from Loonsfoot's furious assault.

Once dressed, the Ukrainian scientist paused only long enough to retrieve a small notebook from the reams of paperwork that littered his workstation at the borehole. Secreting it inside his parka, he then joined Loonsfoot at the stepladder, who by this time had exposed the hatch cover with its small operating handwheel.

Loonsfoot furiously twisted the handwheel counter-clockwise and then pushed the heavy cover upward. A cloud of leaf litter and small dead invertebrates rained down upon them, and cold, dank air spilled into the bunker. The red light of the bunker revealed the first several of the metal rungs that they would have to use to climb upward through the hatch.

The two men then climbed up into the hatch, pulling themselves onto the rungs from the topmost step of the stepladder, and then slowly ascended, with the pale Ukrainian following Loonsfoot. The metal walls and rungs of the hatch were cold and clammy, and the hatch itself was small, damp, and dark, like the interior of a long and narrow grave. Their progress was illuminated only by the red light of the bunker below.

After climbing for about thirty feet, Loonsfoot reached the exit of the escape hatch. His free hand told him that the hatch cover was identical to the one below. Wrenching the handwheel, he pushed upward, but the hatch cover would not budge; lack of use and the accumulated leaf litter and snow, both new and old, kept it wedged firmly in place.

Climbing as high as he could on the last of the metal rungs, Loonsfoot braced his back beneath the hatch cover and then he slowly straightened upward, using his powerful legs, until it seemed as if his back must surely break. At last, the hatch cover grudgingly gave way, swinging upward with its several hundred pound load of snow and debris to reveal the swirling snow above.

After pulling himself out of the hatch and rolling into the snow on the ground, Loonsfoot reached down into the hatch with an arm and helped Lysenko with his exit. The two men pulled their parkas closed around their faces as the heavy snow assaulted them, pelting their flesh that had become unaccustomed to the outside weather with splashy, cold flakes.

Loonsfoot then made his way, from memory, cautiously to the access two-track, with Lysenko close behind. They used all of the scant available cover, careful to keep the ridge between them and the scene of the firefight in front of the bunker door.

No gunshots now sounded. The night was quiet, except for impact of the snow upon their clothing, the howl of the wind high in the branches of the old hardwoods, and the whine of the vibrating instrument lines that adorned the thirty-seven meter high flux tower, the visual centerpiece of their supposed environmental research facility.

As they approached the two-track, Loonsfoot heard the sound of a running car engine and then saw the dull illumination of obscured headlights through the trees. Motioning the Ukrainian scientist to stay where he was, He carefully stalked to within thirty feet of the vehicle. There, he saw the taillights of a small government SUV that was buried in a snow bank and small brush at the edge of the two-track.

Loonsfoot flattened to the ground and crawled forward, keeping his profile as low as possible, and flanked the car on his side of the two-track.

He could tell now, in the reflected glare of the headlights off the snow around them, that the passenger side window had been blown out.

Loonsfoot crawled to the passenger side door of the SUV, and after slowly raising to his feet he cautiously peered inside. There, he saw Wilton and Wenzel slumped against each other, shoulder to shoulder in the front seat, each with his skull partially blown away by the classic 'double tap' of professional assassins.

Both side windows of the vehicle had been blown out, and the front seat was awash with blood. The interior surface of the windshield was covered in a fine spray of blood, hair, bone slivers, and fatty tissue. No helping these two now, Loonsfoot thought grimly.

As quietly as he could, Loonsfoot opened the passenger side door and dragged out the limp body of Wenzel. Leaving the man on his back about ten feet from the car, he then went to the driver side door and repeated the process for Wilton. Loonsfoot turned off the headlights and put the car into neutral, and then, with some effort, pushed it out of the snow bank with his shoulder, back into the two-track. He then quickly backtracked and retrieved Lysenko.

After opening a back passenger door, Loonsfoot assisted the scientist into the car and motioned him to stay down, and stay quiet. Having just seen the bodies of the two dead men in the snow, and their bloody trails from the car where Loonsfoot had dragged them, the pale Ukrainian readily complied.

Loonsfoot slipped behind the steering wheel of the SUV, sitting in the cold, smelly gore that covered the entire front seat. Using the sleeve of his of parka, he smeared enough of an opening in the fine spray covering the windshield to see. He then put the car in four-wheel-drive-low and, as quietly as possible, pushed through the six inches of new, fresh snow on the two-track.

After only going thirty yards, Loonsfoot rounded a corner to find their way blocked by a big, powerful-looking, three-quarter ton pickup with a topper on the back. The massive truck sported a heavy-duty, front-end winch bumper, with large round lights mounted on either side of the winch box.

This was going to be a close thing, Loonsfoot thought grimly. The passenger side of the truck that blocked the road fell off into a bog. He studied the angles.

If he backed up as far as possible and got up as much speed as he could, Loonsfoot thought, hitting the snow bank on the driver side of the pickup and careening off the driver side door, he might just be able to make it without tee-boning a big, old maple some fifteen feet off to the side; he would hopefully glance off the tree back onto the two-track. If he could keep the vehicle upright, Loonsfoot thought fatalistically; it looked like no better than a fifty-fifty proposition. But, the vivid memory of the wild firefight behind them quickly reminded him that there clearly was no other choice.

Putting the vehicle in reverse, Loonsfoot quietly backed up as far as he could to the bend in the two-track, to give him the maximum amount of straightaway. Then, after flicking on the headlights, Loonsfoot put the small SUV back into forward gear and floored the accelerator.

*   *   *   *

Gradually, Sidney Hornberg came back to the land of the not-yet-dead. His groggy vision slowly sharpened as the splashy snow in his face slapped him back to consciousness.

Hornberg was lying back against the branches of the deadfall where the murderous crossfire had thrown him. The pain in his chest from the broken ribs beneath the bullet-resistant vest, as if he had been smashed with a crowbar, kept his breathing to shallow pants, as he struggled desperately to orient himself.

As his senses slowly returned, Hornberg could make out a group of three black-clad men, conversing at the edge of his vision. There was no fight left in him, now. All Hornberg could do was to flee, he knew unconsciously; to escape this nightmare that he found himself trapped in. Run, and run now, his instincts told him, desperately!

Hornberg struggled to push himself upright, away from the deadfall. In so doing, his feet went out from under him in the snow that lay atop the slick leaf litter. He tried to break his fall with his hands, but oddly, only one arm responded. Hornberg fell heavily upon his ruined left arm, and the sudden agony wrenched an involuntary scream of pain from his lips. Let me die now, God, he painfully pleaded in vain as he rolled over onto his back, to the black, snow-filled sky.

At the sound of his anguish, the three black-clad men stopped talking and turned to look in Hornberg's direction. Then they casually walked towards him with their weapons slung, in a loose group, as if they were about to observe the freshly fallen prize of a successful hunt.

"So, Sidney, all of this was so unnecessary, yes?" the tall lead figure said, as he crunched to a stop in the snow at Hornberg's head, with the two others close behind. "That arm, it does not look so good, my friend," he continued in mock concern, jabbing the muzzle of his weapon into Hornberg's left arm above the shattered bone, where the ruined appendage dangled from its remaining tendons and ligaments. Hornberg shrieked in agony. "Be of good heart, Sidney, your suffering will end soon," Gregor continued lightly, as if this was all some grand game, a game being played to the death on the frozen floor of a snowy Upper Peninsula forest.

"Your dead policeman friend over there", Gregor said unemotionally, as he motioned with his weapon in Paul Adams direction on the ridge, where the detective's chilling body was already mounding with snow, "he managed to get in a lucky round before he went down. He killed my longtime friend and comrade, Taimazov, who had been with me in Afghanistan and in many other places," the tall figure continued, bitterly. "Poor Taimazov!" Gregor sighed sadly, with a slow shake of his head.

"But still," Gregor added, after a pause, with sudden apparent conviction and with a slight shrug of his snowy shoulders, "it is the way Taimazov would have wanted to die. The same way all men like us should die, yes, Sidney?" he asked Hornberg, with his head slightly tilted to one side, like an expert instructing a reluctant student.

"Do you remember what I told you of soldiers and sailors before the first time we met, Sidney?" Gregor asked abstractly, with his face animated in the dark hood that covered his head. But Hornberg, his body clenched into a fetal position in the snow in an unconscious attempt to ward off the excruciating pain, heard little of this, and he could not have answered in any case.

"So, Sidney," Gregor continued, matter-of-factly, as if continuing his instruction, "for the moment at least, you still need to breathe, and I still need my Doctor Lysenko. Now where is my man?" Gregor demanded, as he viciously jabbed the muzzle of his weapon into Hornberg's ruined left arm. Hornberg screamed piteously in response.

As if in answer, the three black clad figures suddenly heard the screech of automobile tires and the roar of a revving engine from the two-track entrance to the research facility, above the snow and the wind. The roaring engine noises quickly changed to the alternating pitch and frequency shifts of a vehicle suddenly buried in deep snow. Shouting an epithet, Gregor dispatched the other two men towards the sounds with a quick, loud series of commands in Russian, for he knew with sudden certainty that his prize was trying to escape.

With Gregor still standing at his head, with his back turned to him, as the Russian watched the progress of his men towards the two-track through the blowing snow, Hornberg fumbled clumsily and painfully through his camouflage coveralls with his remaining right hand while the snow blew into his face. He was instinctively trying to find something, anything, to defend himself with, as he had been taught so often over so many years with the Federal Bureau of Investigation.

Hornberg felt the hard outline of his four-inch, heavy-bladed pocket-knife in his back pocket. As he withdrew it with effort, the sudden, ludicrous vision of a small mouse, a mouse standing with the middle finger of one improbable cartoon hand upraised as an owl was about to take up its tiny body in its talons, leapt ridiculously into his now thoroughly insane and tortured mind.

The sudden crackle of two-way radio traffic split the snowflakes at the edge of the old hemlock grove. Gregor had just spoken into the transmitter attached to his coat lapel in Russian in answer, giving his orders, when Hornberg forced his torso off the ground with as much effort as his old, tired back muscles were still capable of. He plunged the small knife deeply into the back of Gregor's left knee joint, and when it stopped, he twisted the blade.

It was Gregor's turn to scream now. As his knee tendons gave way and with his underpinning gone, Gregor fell heavily backward across Hornberg with his weapon thrown above his head, as Hornberg withdrew the knife from the flesh behind his knee. When the Russian had just heavily impacted Hornberg's fractured chest, and even before the instant pain had time to register on his fevered brain, Hornberg swung the knife again, in a backhand motion, with all of his remaining strength.

Hornberg vaguely felt the knife go home into the man's left temple, all the way to the brass clasp in the butt of its heavy handle, with a solid, meaty-yet-hollow sound, as if he had just struck a Halloween pumpkin. Dark blood spurted from around the knife in Gregor's temple, pumped by his rapidly failing heart, as his body arched impossibly backwards on top of Hornberg, covering both of them and the surrounding snow with his hot, red essence.

Finally, Gregor's spasmodic, involuntary bodily actions slowed and then ceased, as Hornberg held him as tightly as he could with his remaining right arm. The two of them, Hornberg and Gregor, the hunter and his prey locked in a final duet of death, now lay intertwined on the snowy forest floor of the Sylvania Wilderness, mounding up with the rapidly falling snow as their bodies began to cool in the quickening storm.

*   *   *   *

KA-WHUMP!

The small Federal SUV righted itself in a cloud of snow on the two-track, jolting the two occupants inside, as Agent Thomas Loonsfoot clung tenaciously to the steering wheel. It had indeed been a close thing, he knew, perspiring profusely, as he glanced into the rear view mirror at the two muddy ruts that marked their progress. The last several feet had been on two wheels only, and only by throwing himself almost completely prone on the front seat had Loonsfoot been able to keep the car from turning over after it had struck a glancing blow off the big maple.

Loonsfoot had been sure that they were hopelessly mired in the snow bank at least once, but his desperate actions had saved them. Desperation, along with a good transmission and four-wheel drive, he thought, with grim satisfaction.

Loonsfoot now quickly drove downhill into the teeth of the snowstorm. Already, the big pickup that had blocked their path had been lost to view in the rear view mirror. He passed the gate that had been flung open wide, and then he turned north onto the icy, snow-covered, macadam county road, fishtailing for several yards.

After regaining control of the small SUV, he saw the taillights of a car that was plunged headlong into the roadside ditch by his side pointing forlornly at the sky. That would be our road surveillance, he realized, bleakly. There would be no help for them from any quarter this night, he knew with certainty, unless he could reach the Tribal police in Watersmeet.

Loonsfoot drove into the storm as fast as he dared on the curvy county road. The wind and the snow were pouring into the driver side of the car through the blown-out side window. He hunkered down behind the steering wheel in an attempt to shelter himself, peering through the small smeared hole in the bloody windshield.

Then, suddenly, they were there, fifty yards behind the small Federal auto. Loonsfoot was sure that it was the big pickup that he had gone around on the Helen Lake two-track, since the trapezoidal arrangement of the headlights and the round lights on the heavy duty winch bumper was both unusual and unmistakable.

Loonsfoot quickly considered his options. Try to make Watersmeet and bring God knows what to his friends and family? Or try to outrun them in the storm? Finally, he followed his instincts. Rolling through the stop sign west onto U.S. Highway 2, he slowed down only enough to navigate the turn and then roared off into the snowy night, away from Watersmeet and any possibility of salvation.

Mile after mile clicked off the odometer, and still the big pickup was behind them, as if pacing them, fifty yards back. Loonsfoot realized that the big truck probably carried more gas than they did. They were tracking Loonsfoot and the physicist like a pack of wolves trails a mortally wounded animal, and they would be there until the Federal vehicle stopped, he knew, whether out of gas or for some other reason.

Finally, Loonsfoot turned north onto a wide dirt road that cut cross-country to State Highway M-64 on the west side of big Lake Gogebic, with the big pickup still behind them, fifty yards away. Loonsfoot knew M-64 well, and he was banking that the occupants in the big pickup did not.

Turning again north on the main highway, Loonsfoot cautiously navigated the first series of curves until he reached the long straightaway to Highway M-28, and then he floored the accelerator. God help us if there is anyone else on this road tonight, he thought morbidly.

As Bingham Bay flew by on his right side, Loonsfoot checked the rear view mirror. The big pickup was gone. This might just possibly work, Loonsfoot thought, optimistically. Then, suddenly, the view in the mirror turned into a solid sheet of flame.

The shock wave from the detonation blew in the rear window of the Federal SUV and picked the car up like a leaf atop a giant wave. Round and round the car skidded, down the icy highway, through a maelstrom of snow, fire, and flying debris. Fire and ice competed for the lives of Thomas Loonsfoot and Sergei Lysenko equally fiercely, like the clash of giants in some ancient rune, competing for the very souls of men.

CHAPTER 13

▼

The ice, or what little was left of it, went out early on Lake Gogebic that spring. Most of the big lake's water had rushed down its outlet to Lake Superior when the dam at the northern Bergland end had been breached the previous winter. The small nuclear blast, trapped between high ground on either side of the lake and muffled by the huge snowstorm that had occurred on that night like an explosion inside a huge feather pillowcase, had beaten the frozen surface of the long, ice-covered lake like a metal drum.

The attendant shock wave following the detonation had killed almost every living thing in the water as it had traveled the length of the lake, fracturing the ice as it went. Finally, the dam at the far end had gone out, relieving the killer pressure gradient to the downstream, hilly woods. The lake ice, no longer supported by water, had sagged downward into the old river channel like a deflated balloon, since it was still rigidly connected to the rocky, shallow shoreline.

At least one hundred forty-seven people had died that night, although the exact total would never be known due to the vast extent of the devastation. It had been the single largest disaster in the recorded history of Michigan's Upper Peninsula, larger by far than the Italian Hall disaster in Calumet during the copper mine strike of 1913. During that tragedy, seventy-three people, including thirty-five children, had been killed at a Christmas party, in a panic presumably caused by mining company men.

Along with lakeside residents, many of the victims of the Gogebic blast had been out-of-state snowmobilers, waiting out the storm in the many lodges and rentals that dotted the lake on both sides. The destruction had been more or less total, almost to the village of Bergland itself.

The official story was that two double tanker trucks, each loaded with extremely dangerous and volatile chemicals, had collided head-on in the vicinity of Bingham Bay on State Highway M-64 during the storm that night. This cover story, together with the fortuitous snow that had kept most of the radioactive contamination along the shores of the lake and that had prevented it from going airborne, had made it relatively easy to quarantine individual shoreline areas. But the scope of the disaster was so large, and the amount of debris so massive, that even now, months later, Federal disaster agencies still had many areas cordoned off.

Many of the individual properties destroyed that night, from small camps that had been in families for generations to massive, million-dollar summer homes of the suddenly rich, would never be able to be rebuilt. The permitting process would be adjusted to ensure that the real reason for rejecting the building applications, the health risks associated with exposure to long-lived radionuclides, would never be revealed.

In the aftermath of the gigantic Lake Gogebic blast, a small underground detonation at the Helen Lake Flux Tower in the deserted Sylvania Wilderness near Watersmeet shortly thereafter had gone completely unnoticed. The thawing spring weather would reveal only a slight depression at the place, with some pipes and conduit sticking out of the ground, like the many others in the Sylvania where the rich industrialists, the original owners, had once had their camps and lodges.

The bodies of the dead Federal agents had been quietly removed and had been returned to their families. The men, the families were told, had been the unintended victims of an overseas intelligence operation that had gone badly awry but that must, at least for now, remain completely secret because of the present exigencies of the 'War on Terror'.

Remarkably, Sidney Hornberg had been found alive, but just barely, beneath the dead body of Colonel Grigoriy Korzhanenk of the Russian GRU, at the foot of a deadfall that overlooked Helen Lake. Although he had been badly frostbitten, the snow and the cold, along with the slowly cooling body of the Russian officer, had reduced Hornberg's respiration and bleeding just enough so that the search team that had been sent out the next day after the storm found him still comatose on the snowy floor of the Sylvania.

Hornberg had immediately been air lifted to the Bethesda Naval Hospital in Washington, D.C., on the direct orders of the President of the United States, where his left arm had been amputated, eight inches above the elbow. Hornberg remained there now, in isolation, with his wife Emma, in attendance, in a persistent, vegetative coma.

In Seattle, 'Operation Thunderbolt', the gravity research project that had caused Doctor Sergei Lysenko, the albino Ukrainian physicist, to be kidnapped, had been a failure. The composition of the ceramic materials necessary for the process was not stable. The Seattle researchers suspected that the pale Ukrainian had neglected to mention some important part of the process, but since he had apparently been killed in the mammoth blast at Lake Gogebic, he was no longer available to question.

And so the project had been scrapped, as previous experiments with 'cold fusion' had been put down. The Federal dollars involved were now desperately needed for expected Middle East military operations and, eventually, for proposed space flight missions to the planet Mars.

Some good, however, had come from the winter disaster in the Upper Peninsula of Michigan, in spite of it all. Barely one month after the Lake Gogebic blast, the President of the Russian Federation, or 'The V-Man', as the President of the United States ingenuously called him, had graciously accepted the President's invitation to again visit him at his Texas ranch. There, in a chilly back room of the ranch after a delightful dinner, the Russian president had been shown the frozen bodies of Colonel Korzhanenk of his country's GRU and the colonel's aide, a Belarusian named Taimazov.

Having 'made his bones' as the head of the KGB before his ascendancy to the top of the Russian political order, the small, nervous man had listened carefully as the Director of the Central Intelligence Agency, who had also been present at dinner, explained through an interpreter how it was that the two bodies on the table before them had come into United States possession. The American President had stood by during the explanation, studying his Russian counterpart's reactions. For his part, the Russian President knew full well what the story portended, and what the American demands would be.

A short time later, the President of the United States and the President of the Russian Federation had made a stunning, joint public announcement. The United States and Russia, the announcement stated, had agreed to completely eliminate all tactical nuclear warheads; all of the suitcase bombs, the artillery shells, the mines, the torpedoes, and all of the other insane nuclear products of the Cold War, on both sides. This would be accomplished by the year 2010, it was proclaimed, with each side retaining just enough strategic nuclear warheads to preclude attack by either. This action, it was announced jointly, was intended to ensure that such terrible weapons could never inadvertently fall into the hands of terrorists.

United States Congressmen, on both sides of the aisle, were ecstatic, and the various news agencies and the public around the world were stunned by the announcement. Television 'talking heads' everywhere now babbled enthusiastically about a new, bright dawn for humanity.

Not stated, however, was the quiet agreement that had been reached between the two heads of state that night in the back room of the President's Texas ranch, before the frozen bodies of the two dead Russian soldiers. There would be no Russian interference in American military moves in the Middle East. The United States would now have a free hand in oil-rich Iraq and Afghanistan; and even in Iran, another oil-rich country that the other two bracketed, if it came to that.

But now, most of the background political drama was behind them on this spring day, as the various state, county, Federal, and tribal officials picked their way along the tortured shoreline of the state park on the west shore of Lake Gogebic. They walked in loose groups, silently viewing the destruction of the past winter with awe and disbelief, and speaking to each other only in low, somber tones.

The stench of rotting fish and small, dead invertebrates was everywhere on this warm spring morning. Uncountable millions of seagulls wheeled in the sky and paraded across the mud flats, for they were the unintended beneficiaries of the death of this big lake. There were already a few flies out, several of the officials noted to each other quietly, but they also knew that it was nothing like what the hot summer would bring, when a billion fly generations would discover the treasure trove of Gogebic's decaying lake life under ideal breeding conditions.

The officials present on this spring day had been invited by the Federal disaster coordinators, who had hoped to gain support from them for the long-term plans for the recovery of the area. Among them, several members of GLIFWC, the 'Great Lakes Indian Fish and Wildlife Commission', a Tribal organization that was responsible for coordinating the Indian harvest of the big lake's prized walleye with the Michigan Department of Natural Resources during the brief spring spearing season, were present.

The Ojibwa fishermen speared the fish at night, during the walleyes' spawning frenzies on the east shore reefs of the big lake, from powerful, modern boats with big spotlights, as permitted by Federally-recognized treaties. Several members of the Tribal Council of the Bad River Band of Ojibwa Indians from Odanah, Wisconsin, a band that traditionally speared the bulk of the spawning fish taken from Gogebic in the spring, were also in the group.

The Ojibwa men and their white counterparts walked silently along the destroyed lakeshore, as terrible scene was replaced by even more terrible scene. Several of the Indians had tears in their eyes as they viewed the destruction of *Agogebik*, the ancient Ojibwa 'Place of Diving'. There would be no spring harvest again in this place, they knew despondently, for at least half of a generation of Ojibwa young men.

And then, some twenty yards further down the shoreline, the most terrible symbolic sight of all presented itself to the Ojibwa men and to the puzzled white officials whom they had accompanied: the massive carcass of a huge fish, bobbing in a slight depression among the shoreline rocks, a fish that was well over eight feet long. Even in its advanced stage of decomposition, floating belly-up and held together only by a few remaining strands of cartilage, the great fish was readily recognizable as a giant lake sturgeon. "*Nah Ma*!" the Ojibwa men muttered, in low tones, between themselves. "*Nah Ma, Nah Ma*!" they chanted together, excitedly.

At the sight of the monstrous fish, one of the members of the Bad River's Tribal Council, a older man, suddenly went into convulsions, as if he were having a spiritual revelation. The old man was well known among the *Anishinabe*, for his father had been a *Djasakid*, a 'Tent-Shaker'. His father had been a mystic who spoke to the spirits, and to the dead, and to the animals, he alone of all the Bad River Ojibwa.

"*Megis*!" the old man cried, as he fell to the ground, trembling violently and retching. "*MEGIS*!" he cried again, splayed out on the ruined ground beneath him, with his arms and his legs twitching and jerking like a hand puppet. "*MEE-GISS*!" he screamed aloud, to the bright, blue sky full of seagulls, as he was being strapped to the backboard in restraints for the trip back to Odanah, in the attending ambulance that was a constant presence now during these dour days on the Lake Gogebic shoreline.

The assembled men on the shore of Lake Gogebic that spring morning watched while the ambulance departed, with its load that consisted of the older Bad River Ojibwa man and all of his tormented, spiritual misery. All present now were silent, both white men and red men alike.

*   *   *   *

In the evening on that same spring day, not very far from Lake Gogebic, Elizabeth Adams and her daughters, and her dead husband's brothers and their families, and state dignitaries from all over Michigan, stood on the shore of the Ontonagon River in the village of that name. They were gathered there to send off her dead husband, Detective Paul Adams of the Michigan State Police, in the manner that he had requested in his Living Will. They were near the mouth of that great river, where *Nah Ma*, the giant lake sturgeon of Lake Superior that were spoken of in the old Ojibwa stories about the area, had once swum during their springtime spawning runs, giving sustenance to the *Anishinabe*.

Detective Paul Adams had been cremated per his final instructions. He was now to be interred in the muddy waters of the springtime Ontonagon

River, a river full of silt from the clay soils of the area and from spring melt runoff from all over the county. His ashes would be then spread all over the Upper Peninsula by the river, in this northern land that he had loved so much.

They stood on the east bank of the river upstream from the swing bridge, at the juncture of the slough and the main branch, where the Bergstrom family dock and fish house had once stood. Against Elizabeth Adams' wishes, a military band had played, the band having been ordered to do so by the President of the United States, personally. Young marines, who could not possibly have even been alive when Paul Adams had been in Asia during the Viet Nam conflict, had rendered an eleven-gun salute to their fallen Michigan comrade. Paul, her husband of so many years, would have probably considered it all rather grotesque, Elizabeth Adams thought tersely.

She had aged considerably in the past few months since Paul's passing, Elizabeth knew. She did not need a mirror to see the effects of his death on her. She stood on the public river fishing pier that the Ontonagon village had considerably put out for them, very early in the season just for this special occasion, with her back bent and her hair completely gray beneath her dignified black hat and veil. Her two daughters, Jenna and Kati, supported her beneath each arm while her husband's eldest brother poured the ashes into the muddy spring turbulence of the Ontonagon River.

Elizabeth sobbed quietly beneath her veil, miserable and distraught. The circle was complete, she knew instinctively in her misery, and all of her childish nightmares had now been fulfilled. She strained her reddened, watery eyes to mark the progress of her husband's ashes through the dark screen across her face. The remains were marked on their journey down the river by a large flower wreath that had been assembled by her children and their friends, quietly and with many tears.

As her husband's ashes were swept by the broad, muddy river towards the waiting azure waters of the great lake, the *Ke-che-gum-me* of the Ojibwa people who had occupied these lands long before the white man arrived on their shores, Elizabeth Adams felt a sad and curious sense of closure. Her fisherman father, Marcus Bergstom, dead for all these many years, now waited to finally meet her husband, the father of her children, as they joined their atoms together in their common watery grave.

And yet, the vast blue lake that now contained the pair of Elizabeth Adams' most important men seemed to mock them all with its icy indifference, as if all of the affairs of mankind were trivial and irrelevant. Elizabeth felt a sudden chill as the spring breeze rolled up the river carrying the cold lake air, and she looked towards her daughters on the pier with concern. They would relocate soon, out of the Upper Peninsula, Elizabeth knew with certainty. Paul would have understood.

Now, a state police bagpiper was playing a sad, melancholy tune. Above the lilting lyrics that wafted across the brown river, lighter than air but heavy with regret, Elizabeth vaguely heard her family minister reciting the immortal words of poet A. E. Housman into the face of the big lake:

Home is the sailor, home from sea:
Her far-borne canvas furled,
The ship pours shining on the quay
The plunder of the world.

Home is the hunter from the hill:
Fast in the boundless snare,
All flesh lies taken at his will
And every fowl of air.

'Tis evening on the moorland free,
The starlit wave is still:
Home is the sailor from the sea,
The hunter from the hill.

EPILOGUE

▼

Far into the future, the rich oral tradition of the Lake Superior Ojibwa will have a new legend. It will be the legend of 'The Eighth Fire', when *Nanabozho*, the Great White Rabbit, the trickster of Ojibwa legend, gave the *Megis* back to his children.

One day, the legend will begin, a young Ojibwa warrior appeared before an old man of the Bad River Band of the *Anishinabe*, near the ancient Ojibwa site of La Pointe in present-day Wisconsin. Here the Great *Megis*, the seashell, had last shone upon them during the Seventh Fire. The young warrior had been gravely wounded, and he was near death. "Help me, old man, for I am the protector of *Nanabohzo*, the Great Rabbit!" the dying young man had implored.

The old man had pity for the warrior and took him in. He tried to make the dying easier for the warrior, for he was clearly crazy; but the young man would have none of it. "Listen to me, old man!" the young warrior demanded, through his great pain. "*Nanabohzo* needs the help of his *Anishinabe* children. He has been in a fight to the death with The Evil One, and he is now also wounded."

The old man bathed the warrior's wounds and picked the shattered glass and woody debris from his charred back. He listened in wonder to the warrior's tale, told in halting, painful fragments as if in a death song.

It began with the great rape of the land by the *Chi-mookomaan*, who had stolen its timber and killed its fish and animals, and who had ripped its mineral wealth from the very bowels of the Mother Earth, leaving nothing behind for the *An-nish-in-aub-ag*, the red race. This part of the story had been told often, and the old man, who had lived through much of it, was well familiar with it.

But this apparently had not been enough for the greedy *Chi-mooko-maan*, the young warrior asserted, haltingly, in his agony. Among the white men, he said, had arisen a truly Evil One, a sorcerer who had so fouled the waters of *Ke-che-gum-me*, the Great Water, that its fish were no longer safe to eat. The Evil One had killed *Agogebik*, the Place of Diving, with a wave of his magical hand. The old man sat mesmerized as he listened to the tale, while he imagined the empty basin some miles east that had once contained *Agogebik*.

His god-like master, *Nanabohzo*, the dying warrior said, had tried to placate The Evil One by pretending to give him the great *Megis*, the seashell, that was the very soul of his children, the *Anishinabe*. But, ever the trickster, *Nanabohzo* had made it so that the *Megis* would vanish into thin air if The Evil One ever tried to make use of its great power.

And that was exactly what had happened. When The Evil One tried to take hold of the great *Megis*, it evaporated, and The Evil One had been left holding only a few worthless grains of sand. Furious, The Evil One then took his revenge, poisoning all the fish in *Ke-che-gum-me* so that the *Anish-inabe* could not eat them, and taking from them *Agogebik*, the Place of Diving.

Nanabohzo then determined to save his children by slaying The Evil One, and a great battle had ensued. Fierce had been the many blows struck during the nighttime struggle, and the whole world had reverberated with the clash of the two titans. But, eventually, *Nanabohzo* had prevailed, and now The Evil One was dead.

Now, the young warrior explained, breathing shallowly since he was very near his own death, *Nanabohzo* needed the help of his *Anishinabe* children. They must care for him, and bind his wounds, and provide him with anything that he requested, as they would for their own dying parents, his young protector said. And in return, the young man had promised, with his eyes now wild, when he had recovered, *Nanabohzo* would show his children the Great *Megis* again. Then the young warrior expired in the arms of the old man, to begin his four-day journey on the road of souls to the spirit land.

They buried the young warrior in the La Pointe Indian cemetery on *Mon-ing-wun-a-kaun-ing*, the Place of the Gold-breasted Woodpecker, or Madeline Island as the white man knew it. His feet pointed to the west, in the direction of the spirit's journey, as Ojibwa tradition demanded, so that he might continue to watch for the next rising of the Great *Megis*.

They built a low spirit house over the young man's grave, with a small window and a ledge, and on it they had placed some food for his journey: maple sugar and some berries, in birch-bark containers. They advised the young man's spirit, which they knew would linger near his body for some time after his death, on the dangers that he might face on his long trek to the Ghost Land.

As the people lingered at the young warrior's grave, the old spirits of the Ghost Land, the Northern Lights of these latitudes, rose and fell in the nighttime sky to the steps of an ancient dance, awaiting their newest member. Then, after planting a flat, sharpened cedar stake with the inverted symbol of his totem, the bear, at his grave to indicate the death of the young protector of *Nanabohzo*, the people sent him off on his long passage to the afterlife.

They found *Nanabohzo* at the place where the young warrior had said that they would. The women of the band, once they had overcome their awe and fear of the strange-looking spirit-man, had bound his wounds and nursed him back to life.

The Tribal Council made another young man, a son of the old man who had found the young warrior and an educated person, the new protector of *Nanabohzo*. He stayed at the Great Rabbit's side forever thereafter. He learned eventually to converse with the pale spirit and provided for all his needs, even the *Chi-mookomaan* scientific instruments and power supplies that his master requested.

So it went on for some years, until *Nanabohzo* recovered from his wounds from his battle with The Evil One and completely regained his strength. And then, one day, in the odd language that the two of them had developed over time between them, the spirit-man requested of his young protector that the Tribal Council be brought to him.

His young protector immediately went to the village and brought back the tribal elders, as he had been bidden. When the old men of the tribe had gathered at the place where the spirit-man was harbored with its curious, red light, *Nanabozho* showed them several mysterious instruments that caused many miraculous things: holes that instantly appeared in solid brick; rocks that floated in the air; and a large, old, empty brass artillery shell that shot away into the night sky, without propellant of any kind.

"These are my gifts to you, my children, in return for your kindness to me," *Nanabozho* said, solemnly, addressing the old men of the tribe as his young protector translated. "Guard them well, for the *Chi-mookomaan* have many more than one Evil One amongst them. Use them as barter to regain your lands, and to clean the poison from *Ke-che-gum-me*, so that the children of the *An-ish-in-aub-ag* may eat its fish again," the pale figure had instructed them.

"Consult with men who are wise in the ways of the *Chi-mookomaan*," the spirit-man had advised them, "for they value these things that I have shown you greatly. Do not allow yourselves to again be cheated, as before," he chided them, "or you and your children will live in poverty and misery forever, in a dark place."

"I leave you now," announced *Nanabohzo*, gravely, "to return to my own home, which is in a far away place. Remember me whenever you see the white rabbit," he said to them, mockingly, in high good humor. And then, he and his young protector were gone, into the night.

The old men of Bad River then did what they had been bidden by *Nanabohzo* on that night of the Eighth Fire. They locked up his miraculous instruments, and they guarded them fiercely. The Tribal Council retained the best lawyers, engineers, and scientists in the Midwest that the combined net worth of the Lake Superior Ojibwa nation, a worth that was considerable in these days with the income from their many casinos and other business interests, could provide for.

Finally, on a cold, rainy spring day on Madeline Island in the Apostle archipelago of Wisconsin, within view of the La Pointe Indian cemetery, officials of the now-united 'Ojibwa Nation of the Superior Lands' had quietly and diplomatically approached the United States government, through Federal Department of Energy representatives, with an interesting and potentially mutually beneficial proposal. Impressed, the Federal officials had immediately returned to Washington D.C. to brief their superiors on these startling, almost unbelievable developments.

As they watched the Federal officials scurry back to the waiting Madeline Island Ferry, the Ojibwa men were not particularly surprised to see a snowshoe hare, still in its dirty, brown-and white transition to its summer coat, hopping around the edges to the cemetery, pausing briefly here and there to nibble on some woody browse. For, among themselves and around the council tables, the Ojibwa called the proposal that they had just made to the United States of America by a certain name, a name that only the *Anishinabe* of Lake Superior knew the meaning of and the reasons for:

It was called *MEGIS.*

978-0-595-38542-3
0-595-38542-7

Printed in the United States
46302LVS00005B/148-354

9 780595 385423